THE LOST SON

A NOVELLA FROM THE BLACK MUSEUM

MARTIN DAVEY

Copyright © 2024 by Martin Davey

All rights reserved.

No part of this book may be reproduced in any form or by any electronic or mechanical means, including information storage and retrieval systems, without written permission from the author, except for the use of brief quotations in a book review.

❦ Created with Vellum

*To everyone who has taken the lift up to the 7th Floor with me,
Happy Christmas.*

CONTENTS

Prelude	1
1. The Resistance	3
2. The Green Tower	11
3. Sid	14
4. Heldra	16
5. Nelson's Loss	20
6. Two True Sons of the East End	25
7. Missing	27
8. The Busker	28
9. The Fox Tail	35
10. The Forgotten Tree	39
11. The Star and the Square	43
12. Found and Lost	44
13. Little Dave	48
14. Wipper and Wasp	58
15. A Face in the Crowd	63
16. Out of Tune	66
17. Oxleas	71
18. The Right Sprite	74
19. The Cat Trap	76
20. Marmite	80
21. All Roads Lead to Trafalgar	82
22. Escape	87
23. A Boy, a Cat and a Reward	89
24. Fangs and a Fiddle	92
25. A Present at Christmas	94
26. Oslo	98
About the Author	101
Also by Martin Davey	103
Afterword	105

PRELUDE

DCI Judas Iscariot of Scotland Yard's secret occult magic division, the Black Museum, was consulting the calendar on the wall of his office and let out a sigh that would have filled the sail of a small boat and pushed it away from the dock. The cause of his consternation? It was already Saturday, November the 30th. December was but scant hours away, and he could feel the cold spectre of yet another Christmas approaching. Or could it be a draught? The radiators on the 7th floor of the New Scotland Yard building were fickle at the best of times.

Judas, cursed by an angry and vengeful God for the death of his only son, and condemned to walk the earth fighting evil wherever he found it, disliked Christmas for obvious reasons. The small matter of being responsible, in part, for the death of the chosen one tended to blight the festive period for him. He was also considerably miffed that the others – let's not forget Pilate, who knew that dear old Jesus was innocent, and the other religious leaders who knew a competitor when they saw one – had not endured punishment to the same extent as Judas. Not nearly as much. No one ever said, 'Oh, you're such a Pilate!' if they'd done something devious.

If he could have pulled down the shutters of the Black Museum and gone on holiday somewhere nice, somewhere hot, somewhere that had seen a run on Christmas trees and turkey, he would have closed the door, locked it behind him and then bribed a motorcycle police officer to get him to the airport. But London's Fae, its magical communities, and the Under Folk, the creatures and the strange types that lived in the Underworld beneath the London Underground, did not celebrate the festive season or knock off for Christmas dinners and office parties. They still needed policing and protection. Christmas was coming. It was inevitable. What it would bring with it this year; only time would tell.

1

THE RESISTANCE

The Forest of Woe. Hisoy Island. Situated east of Bergen and Haugesund West of Norway. 1942.

The magical creatures and the Fae of the forest had joined a long line of the angry, the furious, and the disgusted. The Nazis of the Third Reich had invaded their beautiful island. These grey men, with their lightning insignias, their red flags and their marching songs, had come to their island in force. The cross-tracks and the enormous wheels of their large metal machines had cut the soil to ribbons. They scorched the earth with their fires and felled the young trees to make space to pitch their tents. They ripped up and toppled trees that had grown strong and true for hundreds of years. Then, the men swarmed all over them, chopping their limbs off and building vast piles of logs for their fires. Even the streams and the lakes had been spoiled. Oil and grease from the Nazi war machines found their way into the water table and coated the surface of the streams and the ponds, making rainbow patterns that choked the fish and suffocated the flies and the insects. The forest grew silent. Even the foxes, wolves, elk and deer drifted away.

But there was one woodland creature that was overjoyed that the Germans had come to Hisoy. She was very happy, had never been happier, in fact. Her name was Heldra, and she was a Siren of the Trees. Before the Nazis came, Heldra had preyed on the local fishermen. The Northmen were superstitious types and hard to catch. Heldra had to pray for a storm and rough seas. The Northmen were fine sailors, but when the waves were too high, even for them, they would camp on her island, make a fire, and then drink.

It would not be long before one of them staggered into the woods to relieve themselves. There, she would transform her body and features to become a voluptuous redheaded woman and entice them deeper and deeper into the forest, where she would feed upon them. When the Übermensch of the Reich arrived, however, they were neither cautious nor superstitious. They were so easily distracted that she had feasted to her heart's content these past months. But all good things must end, and twice in the last week, the Norwegian Freedom fighters had scuppered her plans; these silent men in their boats, the true sons of the islands and the lands nearby, had returned.

Heldra realised that her feeding pattern was about to change – *again*. She watched the Northmen run their boats ashore, and she recognised their language. When she saw their weapons, a thought flickered into her dark, twisted mind. Should she alert the Nazis? If she were to raise the alarm, then maybe...just maybe...she might feed on the Germans a little longer. Heldra was greedy, and she had enjoyed these months of the Nazi occupation.

"Why not?" she said to herself.

Heldra crept through the woods towards the nearest

camp. She heard the crackle and the strange noises of the magic boxes that the soldiers carried on their backs long before she saw the first sentry. When she was near enough, Heldra uttered her magic words and felt the cool night breeze flow over her fresh human skin. She always looked forward to the men's wide-eyed expression when they saw her appearing through the branches. It excited her, and she felt powerful. But something else was nearby that night, something like her, and she froze.

It was a Fosse Grimm, a Woodland Sprite known throughout the forests as Bosk. She had seen it many times before, wandering here and there in search of the perfect branch to turn into a bow for its fiddle. Mostly, the Fosse Grimm were harmless and kept themselves to themselves, but tonight, Bosk had sought her out.

"Siren?" whispered Bosk.

Heldra remained still and quiet. The sentry nearby sensed something and brought his weapon up to his shoulder.

"Siren! Do not alert them to the Northmen and their boats," hissed Bosk.

"Who are you to tell me what to do, sprite?" she said.

The sentry squinted and tried to pierce the darkness with his eyes. Had he heard something, or were his eyes playing tricks on him again? He was not sure and did not want to drag everyone from their warm beds for a false alarm. But then again, he did not want his *sergeant, a real bastard from Bavaria, to shoot him in the face for not alerting the men if there was something in the woods.

"Siren. You have had your way with these Nazis for months now, but the forest needs to be free now. The other spirits have not fared as well as you – their homes have been flattened, and their food source is all but gone. If you wake the Nazis and they fight the Northmen, many of our kind will die, and we will almost certainly be pushed out of the forest. Let these jackbooted thugs slumber and let the men of these lands kill them in their sleep. Life will return, and you will feast again," said Bosk.

The sentry concluded that the noise he had heard was just a bird or a mouse, lowered his weapon and walked away. Heldra watched her next meal disappear, turned herself back into her true form and crouched down so that she could see Bosk properly. He was short, as all sprites are, and he carried his precious fiddle and bow in a sling over his shoulder. The Fosse Grimm had long dark hair and dazzling bright blue eyes, and he could sing songs to make a creature happy, sad, brave, want to howl at the moon, and just about anything else it wanted them to do. That was why they were dangerous and to be avoided.

Heldra did not like the Fosse Grim very much. They had more strings to their bow than she did. Heldra could make you want to love her, but that was it. So, she reasoned with the sprite.

"So you say, Bosk. But you have not spent the long months when the night lasts forever hungry and alone, as I have. What have the others done for me?" she said.

"They do not poison the water and fell the trees for warmth, Heldra. They do not dig and chop and spoil. Let them fight their fight, and they will be gone in their boats before the sunrise," said Bosk.

"And if I refuse, Fosse Grimm?" said Heldra.

"If you act for yourself and yourself only, I will sing a song that will turn the entire forest against you. The birds and the bats will sing to you all day and all night so that you have no peace. The wolf and the bear will root you out and attack you, and the trees will no longer shelter you, Heldra. Think about it," said Bosk.

Heldra was hungry, but the Fosse Grimm's threat hung in the air between them, and she knew in her black heart that he meant what he said, and if she persisted, the other creatures would turn on her in a trice.

"Do we have an agreement?" said Bosk.

There was no answer because the Siren was gone.

The Norwegian Freedom Fighters attacked just before dawn. They caught the Nazis unawares and killed everyone in the camp. They liberated and removed all of their weapons and precious radios to the waiting Norwegian boats. The tents and the stores, the sleeping bags, and all the fuel they could carry were taken away and divided amongst the men. The leader of the Norwegian task force found the Germans' secret papers and their code books; he wrapped everything in oiled silk packages so that they would not be ruined by the water or the snow and carried them away, pressed to his chest like a newborn babe. The dead German bodies were tipped into a large open grave and then covered with earth. After the freedom fighters had finished covering their tracks and piling green ferns and snow on top of the site, any evidence or sign that the Nazis had been there was gone. The forest breathed out, and the sigh caused the branches of all the trees to sway, and snow to fall.

One of the freedom fighters, a local man, wise in the ways of woodland lore, heard the trees talking. They spoke of peace and of victory, and it was just then that something occurred to the man. The war and the Nazi occupation had forced the King of Norway and his family into exile in London. Much in the same way that the animals and the creatures of the forest had been pushed out by the Germans.

But now, the island was finally free of them. It was only a little piece of Norway, but it was a beginning.

There had been rumours that the King's spirits were failing. So the fighters decided that the news of their victory on Hisoy would be accompanied by a gift for the King, something to remind him of his home, the woods, forests, hills and streams of Norway. They would send a tree to London for him, a tree at Christmas. It would be a symbol that the land was near and waiting. They picked the biggest tree they could transport safely, cut it down, secured it to the deck of the largest boat and prepared to set sail.

Heldra watched and listened to the men talking. The freedom fighters were misguided. Their King was in another country; how would they get the huge tree to him across the wide sea? And, more importantly, why? What difference would it make? She was just about to turn away from the men when she saw Bosk. The Fosse Grimm had slipped unseen aboard one boat and was busy making himself at home in the branches of the tree the men had just stowed on the deck. Heldra was confused. Where was he going? Why was he leaving? She decided to find out.

Bosk had found himself a lovely little place to hide and was absentmindedly adjusting the tension on his bow when he heard her creeping through the branches.

"Where are you heading, Siren?" said Bosk.

"I was about to ask you the same thing, sprite," said Heldra.

"I am going across the sea to where the people are, to listen to their stories and their songs," said Bosk.

"Are there many people there, sprite?" said Heldra.

"Yes, there are," said Bosk.

"Well then, I shall go to where the people are too, Fosse

Grimm. If the feast will not come to me, I shall go to it," said Heldra.

Bosk placed his bow down on the trunk of the tree and stared at the Siren.

"I travel so that I might learn new songs. You are going somewhere new so that you can kill and then feast!" Bosk exclaimed.

"And what, pray tell, is wrong with that?" Heldra snapped.

"This island is small, Siren; there is nothing here to trouble you, and the fishermen will return. Out there, the islands are vast, and there are creatures there that will kill you instead," said Bosk.

"Kill me?" said Heldra.

"Never doubt it, Siren," said Bosk.

"You say that to frighten me, but I am as old as these woods, sprite, and I will go where I choose," said Heldra.

"One of my songs will change your mind in an instant, Siren. But, you are indeed a creature of the woods, as am I, and I hold no dominion over you. But mark my words; the further you go, the more dangerous it will be. The humans have teeth now, and they are not fools," said Bosk.

Heldra did not reply, and Bosk went back to plucking on the strings of his fiddle and humming a sad, haunting melody. Then the boat's engine growled, the deck beneath them vibrated, and the propeller churned the dark water until it was white. The captain of the vessel turned his wheel, and they set off into the darkness, hoping not to attract the attention of a German launch or a spotter aircraft of the Luftwaffe.

Heldra felt uneasy; she was breaking her bond with the forest. But there was also a small part of her that was excited. She found herself a branch far away from Bosk and settled down to sleep.

2

THE GREEN TOWER

The Nordmarka Forest Oslo, Norway November 2023

The weather has been unseasonably harsh. It has been snowstorm after snowstorm. The forest creatures can sense that there is more to come from the heavens, and they stay warm and dry hidden away in their tunnels and holes, waiting for the wind and the sun to turn their world green once more. The only creature stupid enough to have ventured out into the white void today is a man dressed for the uncompromising weather. Temperatures are low, and the wind chill is high. He is wearing sturdy boots that the manufacturer promises are 100% waterproof, thick socks, thermal long johns, two base layers, and a parka coat with a grey fur-lined hood. For all his insulation and hi-tech fabric, he is still bloody cold.

The man's name is Mons, and he is the Head Forester for Nordmarka, a beautiful forest just north of the city of Oslo. He is on his monthly pilgrimage to visit his two champion trees. He has given them names. His favourite is called the

Green Tower because it is the largest and greenest. The other is called the Green Spear because it is the perfect shape for a Christmas tree. Some of his fellow foresters laugh at him because he takes this job so seriously, but Mons does not care about that. He loves the great forest and enjoys this time of the year the most. Nordmarka has been entrusted by the Norwegian Royal Family and the people of Norway to grow the tree to be sent to London as a gift for the people of Great Britain, to honour them for their support during the Second World War.

A ferry will transport it to Britain where it will stand proudly in Trafalgar Square, in the very heart of London and beneath Lord Horatio Nelson's gaze. People will sing Christmas carols around it, and millions of tourists from all four corners of the earth will join with revellers and party-goers to celebrate the festive season. Mons knows that most of the visitors will be unaware of the tree's heritage, but it is important to him he does his best. When he reaches the Green Spear, he is shocked to find that the tree has given way to the weight of the snow and the strength of the wind. The tip of the tree has broken off, and there are vast gaps in the branches, so big that he can see the sky through them. Mons panics and makes his way down the slope and away from the blunted spear. When he reaches the Green Tower, he is relieved to find that his favourite is still standing tall and firm.

Mons hugs the trunk of the tree and thanks the spirits of the forest for keeping the tree safe. Then he removes the can of green spray from his rucksack and shakes it until he can hear the ball-bearing rattling inside, and draws a smile on the trunk of the tree. It is ready to be felled. When he gets back to the Ranger Station, he will inform the authorities that Nordmarka is ready for the ceremony and that they can liaise with the British Ambassador in Oslo to set a time and date.

3

SID

Sid was an easy lad to love. He was studious and wanted to make his mother and father proud of him. He played lots of sports and did not smoke or vape. Sid drank with the boys, but not too much. His online presence was minimal, and he was not prone to moods or sudden extremes in behaviour. When his parents told him that Sid's father had been offered the post of British Ambassador and that they were going to be leaving their home in Richmond at the end of his school's summer term and moving to Oslo, Sid did not have a meltdown or throw his television into the swimming pool. Instead, he shook his father's hand and told him he was very proud of him. They had a leaving party at their home in July. The daylight hours belonged to the adults and the Government types. Dusk heralded the start of Sid's party, and lots of his friends came, and they partied hard.

Over the course of the evening, there were two fights – one of them boy on boy and the other girl on girl. Afterwards, there was much making up and crying, and that was just the boys. Sid looked on and knew that the altercations had been fuelled by one too many jelly shots, and then, at midnight, one of his girlfriends, a pretty girl called Jenny, whisked him away to the downstairs cloakroom and gave him a special going-away present. In the morning, the cleaners arrived with their industrial party evidence-erasing machines, and by the time his parents returned from their overnight stay in a local six-star hotel, the house was just as they had left it.

Oslo turned out to be the perfect city for Sid. The International School was nearby, and luckily, there were no problematic sorts in any of his classes. The skiing and snowboarding were incredible, he managed not to embarrass himself playing hockey, and he discovered boxing. His father and mother were kept incredibly busy, and Sid didn't see them as much as he had done in Richmond, but he understood that the first year in the post was always going to be crazy for them, and he just got on with his life and supported them when they needed it.

One such request for his support arrived in early November. He was asked to stand in for his mother because she had yet to recover from a stubborn bout of the Flu. The British Ambassador was scheduled to attend a ceremony in the Nordmarka on November 8th. A giant Christmas tree had been selected as a gift for the British people, and it was going to be felled and sent to London. Sid, of course, agreed to go in his mother's stead.

4

HELDRA

When Heldra reached the Nordmarka forest in the summer of 1945, she felt as though she had finally found somewhere to call home. She liked the woodland and the streams, there was plenty of space, and there were magnificent trees everywhere in which to hide and sleep. She located the largest, and settled in. The forest always had a steady supply of visitors. There were hikers, campers, skiers and even swimmers! Heldra picked only the weakest, and those who exercised on their own. The disappearance of a cross-country skier could result from a fall; or faulty equipment; or it could be because of an encounter with one of the wild animals that roamed the Nordmarka. No one suspected that there was a Siren living in the woods, and Heldra, who had changed a great deal since the days of Bosk and the Nazis, was discreet.

The Ambassador's team arrived at the Forest Ranger's hut on the 8th of November, 2023 and received a safety brief from the Head Forester. He inspected their clothes. One of the previous Ambassador's aides had arrived for the tree-felling ceremony the year before wearing a pair of very expensive Italian loafers and a windbreaker. He had nearly frozen to death in the time it took for him to walk across the car park. Ever since then, they expected guests for the ceremony to dress accordingly. Sid was wearing his snowboarding trousers and a plain grey snowboarding jacket, gloves, and a dark blue Carhartt beanie on his head. His father had already told him that when the ceremony started, he should remove it. Sid had taken along a comb and some wax for that moment, to tame his thick and unruly dark hair.

The Head Foresters team had set out several markers along one firebreak in the forest so that everyone could get to the tree without getting lost. Sid asked if he could travel with the two Foresters. They were going to drive up to the tree in one of the new fast-track snowmobiles; he'd seen them roaring through the forest and wanted to try it out for himself. Mr Beaker, the Ambassador's Head of Security had been reluctant at first, but Sid was a careful and trustworthy lad, so he gave authorisation.

The snowmobile was everything that Sid expected it to be, and the two Foresters were very proud of it and wanted to show off its capabilities. It threw Sid about like a rag doll in a washing machine, but he enjoyed the ride enormously. When they reached the clearing and parked the snowmobile, Sid tumbled out to stretch his legs before the massed ranks of the Nordmarka PR teams and his father's retinue arrived to set up camp. The clearing was quiet, and the two Foresters told him they were going to have to leave him for a few minutes because there was a dead elk lying in the middle of a track used by hikers. Sid waved them off and went for a short walk.

Heldra did not like the fast metal boxes. They were noisy, and they reminded her of the Nazis and the island.

Whenever they appeared, she would climb back into her tree and wait until they had passed by. Her tree was magnificent, tall and strong, and even when the wind brought the bitter cold, she was safe and sound, and warm. Heldra scanned the clearing. The metal moving box was still there, but the clearing was empty and quiet. Then she saw the young man, and her stomach growled. He was young and looked fit and strong. He looked tasty. Heldra looked back down the path that led to her tree. There was nothing approaching. No more boxes, no more people. So, she dropped from her tree and padded after the boy.

Sid was really enjoying living in Norway. He had always thought that his father would get one of the plum positions in South America first, but he'd learned that his mother and father wanted him to finish his education in Europe before asking him to follow them further afield. He was incredibly grateful for that. Oslo was a fantastic place, and he wanted to stay there for another year or two. His mother had plied Sid with coffee and orange juice that morning. Her maternal instincts had kicked in, and he could tell that she was feeling responsible for him having to attend the ceremony. The upshot of the extra coffee was that Sid was really feeling the call of nature, and as he was on his own and far away from the cameras, he found a fallen tree behind which to answer that call.

Heldra watched the young man closely. He moved more urgently. He was looking around more often. The young man appeared to be searching for something. Heldra smiled; the young man wanted to make water and was looking for somewhere to remove his clothing. This was perfect. She wouldn't even have to change her appearance. A quick bite to the back of the neck and he'd go limp. Then she would drag him into the tree and devour him at her leisure.

Sid found the perfect place for his emergency ablutions. The Foresters had built a small pyramid using dead trees and logs. Sid positioned himself so that he was not visible from the clearing above, unzipped his fly and urinated. He was straightening his coat and checking his zip when he heard a twig snap behind him. He turned around quickly but not quickly enough, and something slammed into him, smashing his head into a log. He heard a cross between a snarl and a soft voice whispering in his ear, and then he felt sharp points biting into the back of his neck, and he passed out.

Heldra picked the young man up. He was a lovely, reassuring weight; there was clearly plenty of meat on his bones, but she lifted him easily and bolted for her tree. She could hear some more of the metal moving boxes coming, and she was not about to lose her dinner. She reached the clearing just as the first of the cars turned off at the firebreak. Heldra leapt up, clearing the first few branches with ease, and then climbed up the tree, being careful not to dislodge any of the snow. When she was halfway up, she placed the body of the young man inside a den that she had built for herself using discarded branches and twigs. Anyone looking up the tree would not have been able to see it; the camouflage was perfect.

5

NELSON'S LOSS

Sid's father was called Nelson. His grandfather was a devotee of the works of the celebrated and revered king of historical naval fiction, Patrick O'Brian. Sid often made jokes about his father's name, and when he was younger, he thought it highly amusing to make eye patches out of tea towels and old rugby socks and make a nuisance of himself, bumping into the furniture and disrupting his father's work. Nelson, being a good father and an easy-going chap did not rise to his son's constant baiting and answered the boy in kind, slipping his arm out of his sleeve and pretended to have lost the limb somewhere. They played a lot, even though Nelson was busy enough for two grown men.

The Head Forester approached Nelson, and after they had exchanged the customary greetings, he led the Ambassador through the trees to the edge of the clearing and showed him *The Green Tower*.

"Now, that is a sight to stir all the senses. A truly magnificent tree!" exclaimed Nelson.

The Head Forester was pleased. Very pleased.

"We tend the trees for several years, Ambassador, and over time, we weed the weaker ones out and try to give trees like this one more room. We remove some of the other trees from around them so that they get more light and can flex their branches," said the Head Forester.

Nelson had read as much as he could about the ceremony and asked the Head Forester numerous questions regarding growing the tree and then finally choosing the right one. The Head Forester enjoyed the Ambassador's questions and was secretly delighted that the Ambassador appeared so engaged. They talked for another twenty minutes before Nelson noticed that the rest of his team were fidgeting and stamping their feet to keep warm.

"I could talk about this all day, but I feel that you and I might be the only ones left here in the clearing if we did. I think we should move on and cut this lovely tree down, don't you?" said Nelson.

The Head Forester smiled and bowed slightly, not in deference to the Ambassador but more a nod of understanding. Nelson was shown to the safe standing area and was pleased to see camping chairs for the distinguished guests next to the coffee and pastries. Nelson was happy to take a seat and drink some of the delicious coffee, but he noticed Sid was not anywhere to be seen. He called over one of the Embassy staff and whispered to him, enquiring as to the whereabouts of his son. The ceremony was about to take place in earnest. The staffer shook his head; he had not seen him since the drive to the forest earlier that morning.

The Head Forester cleared his throat theatrically, and Nelson and the rest of the staff stopped what they were doing and stood to attention, dropping their plates of half-eaten pastries onto the chairs and hurriedly wiping the sweet powder from their lips.

"Ambassador, friends and fellow Foresters, it gives me the greatest pleasure to welcome you all here today and to continue to show our respect and gratitude to the people of Great Britain for their help, assistance and sacrifice during the Second World War. We hope that this tree will stand as proudly in Trafalgar Square under the eyes of one great Nelson as it does today in the presence of our very own Nelson, the Ambassador of Great Britain in Oslo," said Mons.

He had never been a brilliant speaker and hoped that his reference to Nelson had not been too heavy-handed. He needn't have worried.

"I, my family and my people thank you all for this wonderful gift. It will light up London and continue to show how close our two countries are to this day. The King has written to me and asked me to say that he hopes our friendship will endure for many more years to come," said Nelson.

The Head Forester nodded once again, unclipped a walkie-talkie from his belt, pressed the receiver and instructed the man with the biggest chainsaw in the world to do his duty. The saw sputtered into life then let out a throaty roar. Nelson looked around for his son, but there was still no sign of him.

Heldra heard the noise at the base of her tree then felt the vibrations through the trunk as the chainsaw bit. She panicked. Her tree was being destroyed. Snow was falling from the branches. Then she felt her tree shudder, and she thought she heard it groan as it leaned to one side. She felt like roaring and dropping to the ground to attack the vandals responsible for this sacrilege, but she began to feel out of sorts. Her connection to the land and its power was being severed. The tree lurched even more violently, and Heldra felt like vomiting. She was losing her grip on this world. Heldra grabbed the boy by the neck again and thought about fleeing, but at that moment the tree fell, and she and her meal were bound to it forever. They would not be free again until the tree was anchored to the ground.

Nelson and his team clapped and marvelled at the skill of the tree surgeon. It had fallen in exactly the right place. Nelson felt slightly uneasy at the culling of such a beautiful living thing but reassured himself that it was a symbolic gesture. He wished Sid had been there to see it with him. They loaded the tree onto a flat-backed lorry and secured it with hundreds of straps. Nelson sent a couple of his staff to search for Sid and ask him politely to make an appearance; the lorry would depart soon to avoid the local traffic near Oslo.

Nelson couldn't recall when the first wave of panic hit him. He had always relied on his British stiff upper lip to deflect most of his worries, but Sid was his son, and Sid was not prone to disappearing or wandering off without letting someone know what he was doing. Mr Beaker tried to reassure the Ambassador that Sid would be located soon. The Head Forester, sensing the British Ambassador's growing feelings of anxiety and fear, detailed his men and women to fan out and search the forest.

The lorry and the tree departed an hour later. There was no sense holding it back any longer, and the haulage company responsible had already been berated by the ferry company and told in no uncertain terms that if they did not load the tree onto the ship by that evening's high tide, that they could get it to London themselves.

Mr Beaker spoke with the local police, and soon, the forest was alive with the beams of torches and the squawking of multiple radios. At midnight, Mr Beaker convinced the Ambassador that he should go back to the

Embassy; he was needed there, and it was his responsibility as the Embassy's head of security to make sure that the Ambassador complied. Nelson argued he was a father first and that his son might be hurt, but Mr Beaker would not be denied, and Nelson was whisked back to the Embassy to tell his wife that their son was missing. Neither of them slept that night, and they slept little the following night or the one after that. There was no sign of Sid. The police combed the forest with the help of the military. The city of Oslo itself was turned upside down and given a good shake, but there was still no sign of him.

6

TWO TRUE SONS OF THE EAST END

London. Trafalgar Square. December the 1$^{st.}$

"I saw him do it with my own eyes! He was driving down Fifth Avenue in New York, traffic everywhere, sirens blaring, roadworks and diversions, and there he was, driving one of the big sixteen-wheelers with one hand on the wheel and rolling a cigarette in the other. That, my friend, is impressive," said Charlie.

Charlie was Dave's co-driver. They were in the cabin of Dave's truck waiting for the Metropolitan Police's motorcycle outriders to persuade two of London's black cab drivers to move their cabs out of the way to avoid being flattened by an enormous Christmas tree. The drivers of the black cabs were giving the police a piece of their minds, and it took a further five minutes for the police to persuade them that moving was in their best interest. Finally, one of the police officers looked up at Dave and gave him the thumbs up.

"You think rolling a cigarette with one hand and driving

up Fifth Avenue is impressive do you? Well watch this," said Dave.

Charlie smirked. Dave turned the key in the ignition, checked his mirrors, then performed the neatest and swiftest reverse of a large flat-backed lorry into a tight space ever seen in the centre of London.

"If the pigeons had hands, they would have clapped!" said Dave.

"Not bad," said Charlie.

The crane operators were impressed with Dave's driving too. They wasted no time in removing the straps that held the tree secure, and within 30 minutes they had it upright and standing in an enormous wooden container packed with soil. Support lines were attached to the tree and pinned to the ground using brutish-looking bolts and heavy metal plates. The tree was well and truly anchored.

Charlie and Dave took a selfie in front of the tree and then drove back to Dagenham. Later, in their local pub, they would regale the other locals with tales of how they, two sons of the East End, were responsible for bringing Christmas to the city.

7

MISSING

Mr Beaker, formerly of the Intelligence Corps and then Special Branch, had spoken with his contact at the Home Office in London and informed him he was going to speak with a good friend at Interpol. He was going to call in a favour. Beaker admired and respected his boss but the disappearance of the Ambassador's son, Sid, was slowly but surely destroying Nelson Campbell. The Ambassador had stopped eating properly, and he hardly slept. Dark circles had formed under his eyes and he had become impatient and cranky, which are not ideal qualities in an Ambassador.

On the 2nd of December, the Oslo Police Department's biggest-ever manhunt was terminated. The search had produced no leads, and the whereabouts of Sid Campbell, the son of the British Ambassador in Oslo, was still a mystery. The following day, Sid was placed on the missing persons' register, and his details were shared with every law enforcement bureau and police force in Europe.

8

THE BUSKER

Bosk, the Fosse Grimm, had worn his favourite disguise. Today, he was a busker, a singer of songs, a modern-day bard and a wandering troubadour. He was wearing dark blue jeans, Red Wing boots with worn-down soles, a big warm parka coat and a black bobble hat. His bow and fiddle were strapped to his back, and he looked every inch the fashionista. Bosk had been spending his nights in the Frognerparken in Oslo. It was a lovely park with a couple of museums on the grounds and a sculpture called the Monolitten that he liked to sleep under. The last two weeks had been very rewarding, and he had made quite a tidy sum from his singing, but he had grown restless and now wanted to see the trees and the open fields again. His next port of call was going to be the Viking Ship Museum in Huk Aveny. There were people there who still yearned for the old days and the traditional ways.

He set off from the park at dawn and found a coffee shop open near the British Ambassador's residence on Thomas Heftyes gate. After a leisurely breakfast and two strong cups of coffee, Bosk paid his bill and headed off towards the E18 road. It would take him up to Dronning Blancas Vei, and from there, it was just a hop, skip and a jump down the road to Huk Aveny and the Vikingskipshuset.

He was just passing the Ambassador's residence when he heard two young ladies talking outside. They were in deep conversation. Something terrible had happened in the Nordmarka. A young boy, the Ambassador's son, had disappeared; no trace of him had been found, even after a long search. Some people had suggested that he could have been attacked by a wild animal, maybe a wolf or a bear. Bosk stopped in his tracks. The two women continued their conversation but did not see Bosk standing nearby. He felt a strange sensation then, and the little voice in his head told him he was standing outside the British Ambassador's residence for a reason. Bosk listened to his inner voice, and it reminded him that a certain creature – a creature that feeds on humans – lived in that forest.

The young women moved to a bench on the opposite side of the street and sat down. Bosk followed them and pretended to read some of the public notices in a glass-fronted case attached to the wall behind the bench.

"It's a disaster for the family," said one woman.

"Their only son, gone, just like that," said the other.

"The police have turned the city upside down, no trace at all. There's a rumour going around that it might be one of those serial killers and that no remains will be found, if you understand me," said the first woman.

"Eaten?" said the second woman.

"So they say. The Ambassador has gone crazy, poor man," said the first woman.

Bosk didn't need to hear anymore. He would not be going to the Viking Ship Museum today; instead, he would head to the Nordmarka.

When he got there, the forest was silent and still. He sensed it knew it had been the scene of a heinous crime, and it felt guilty. Bosk found a secluded dell. He looked around to make sure that he was alone, then he transformed.

It felt good to be his true self once more. To feel the grass underfoot and the ferns brushing against his legs as he walked. The forest recognised him; it recognised his sort, a sprite, a friend to the forest, and soon, he heard the voices of the animals on the wind and to see the shapes and the forms of the Fae in the mist. Bosk walked on, and before long he came across a stream and stopped beside the flowing crystal-clear water. It had been some time since he had been able to just sit and enjoy the sounds, and he was loath to break the spell they cast over him, but he needed to find out if the boy's disappearance had anything to do with the Siren. So, he reached for his case and took out his fiddle and bow. At first his bowing and fingering were clumsy and awkward but he soon found his rhythm, and the melody improved. He sang.

His song was a plea to all living things nearby. He asked politely and in friendship for the location of the Siren and it was not long before he learned what he needed to know. Bosk stood up and placed his instrument back inside his case. Then he turned to the south and set off towards the remains of the Siren's tree.

Bosk reached the clearing and saw the stump. He could see that the tree had been mighty and must have stood very tall indeed. He reached out and placed the palm of his hand at the centre of the trunk, and it was not long before he heard the tree whispering to its kin nearby. Bosk called out to the tree, and after exchanging the required civilities, the tree told its sorry tale. It had been occupied by the Siren, and she had stored many of her victims in its branches.

Great violence had been perpetrated, and much blood had been spilt on branch and bark.

"Where is she now?" asked Bosk.

"Gone, across the sea," said the tree.

"Across the sea to where?" said Bosk.

"To London," said the tree.

"Did she go alone?" said Bosk.

"No, she took a boy with her," said the tree.

Bosk thanked the tree for the information and then headed back to Thomas Heftyes gate. He had some news for the Ambassador.

Bosk changed back into his busker's disguise at the edge of the forest and started walking back into the city. As he walked, he considered a number of things. What was he going to say to the Ambassador? Why was he getting involved? How far was he prepared to go to find the boy and bring him home? There was a lot to mull over.

He reached the British Embassy an hour later, having walked some of the way and having been given a lift by a lovely old lady for the rest of the brief journey. As the lady chatted about her dog and the cost of living, Bosk nodded politely and joined in when prompted, but his mind was elsewhere, and he fancied the lady was disappointed with his conversation and more than happy to drop him off at the Embassy. Before she drove away, he thanked her for her kindness and placed a charm upon her. She would suddenly win a prize on the State Lottery, something life-changing perhaps. Bosk walked through the gate and up to the door of the Embassy. He pressed the buzzer on the keypad marked 'General Enquiries'. He had decided it was his duty to rescue the boy because he had allowed Heldra to leave the island.

A few seconds later, the door juddered an inch and a

harsh robotic buzzer sounded. Bosk placed his palm upon the door and pushed. The interior of the Embassy was much more glamorous than the exterior. A white glass sphere of light hung down from the ceiling on a brass chain thick enough to pull up an anchor. A red carpet stretched away from him, disappearing underneath a pair of highly polished wooden doors with matching brass handles. To his right, a young woman sat behind a lovely oak desk that was large enough to play ping-pong over. A lamp on the desk at her elbow had a forest-green shade and produced just enough light for Bosk to see that the young woman had one hand on the desk and the other hovering over a panic alarm button, he presumed.

"Hello, my name is Bosk. Is the Ambassador here today? I may have some information regarding his son," said Bosk.

The young woman's hand moved quickly, twice in succession, and Bosk realised that he would not be meeting with the Ambassador himself first; rather, he would meet someone from the Ambassador's security team. Bosk had already considered this scenario and was more than happy to play along.

The man who sauntered through the wooden double doors was called Mr Beaker, and he invited Bosk to follow him down a narrow corridor. Bosk could tell that they were heading away from the front door, and when Mr Beaker took one flight of steps downwards, Bosk knew that he was heading into the bowels of the British Embassy.

Mr Beaker opened a door on the right-hand side of the corridor and ushered Bosk inside. A small table and two chairs were the only furniture. It was quite a sad room, in fact. Bosk sat down and placed his fiddle case on the floor by his feet. Mr Beaker adjusted his tie and stared into Bosk's eyes.

The Lost Son

"May I have your name and address, please?" said Mr Beaker.

Bosk reached across the table calmly and gently took hold of Mr Beaker's pen, plucked it from his grasp and laid it down on the paper in front of them both.

"I'll tell you everything you need to know, Mr Beaker, but we won't need a pen or paper," said Bosk.

Mr Beaker did not react to this unusual incursion into his own personal space. On any other day and at any other time, he would have suggested in no uncertain terms that the visitor kindly keep their hands to themselves. But there was something reassuring about Bosk, something that made him feel comfortable. And so it was that Mr Beaker, the Head of Security for the British Ambassador in Oslo, made a call and then vacated the interview room with his visitor and escorted him to the Ambassador's private chambers. Moments later, Bosk was sitting across the table from the Ambassador.

The man in the chair opposite Bosk was clearly on the verge of a nervous breakdown. There were dark circles underneath his eyes; he fidgeted, had developed a slight squint in his right eye, and his breath was fetid.

"Forgive me, but what is the correct honorific to address you by?" said Bosk.

"Please, just use Ambassador."

"Ambassador, my name is Bosk. First of all, may I say that I hold no position in any law enforcement agency, nor do I hold a private investigator's licence, but I can find missing people. I have reason to believe that your son has been taken to London. I ask for no payment or fee to locate and then return your son," said Bosk.

Mr Beaker leaned forward and whispered something into the Ambassador's ear.

"What do you want in return, Mr Bosk?" said the Ambassador.

"I will not ask for political favour or influence, Ambassador. If that is your concern. To be truthful, there is nothing you have that I want," said Bosk.

The Ambassador twitched, and Bosk saw him scratch at the knuckle of the little finger on his left hand.

"I have no idea who you are, Mr Bosk. But If you have come here to torment me and my wife, believe me, there is nothing you can do to hurt either of us any further because we are already in Hell. So please, if this is some newspaper stunt or the beginning of some plot to blackmail us, desist now; there is nothing to be gained from any further lies or false promises," said the Ambassador.

Bosk watched as a single tear ran down the Ambassador's face and dripped onto the desk. The man was nearly broken, and Bosk pitied him.

"I shall stay in contact with Mr Beaker," said Bosk and stood up to leave.

The Ambassador's head dropped ever so slowly until his forehead rested on the desk and as Mr Beaker escorted Bosk back to the entrance, he heard the Ambassador sob.

9

THE FOX TAIL

Heldra woke with a start. There was noise everywhere. Loud, invasive noise! Horns and screeching, banging and crashing coming from everywhere all at once, and she clasped her hands over her ears to shut it all out. It took a while for her to become accustomed to it. The forest was always quiet. This place, wherever this place was, was noise, pure noise. Heldra climbed further up the tree until she felt brave enough to peek out through the branches. The first thing she saw was a stone man standing on a high column. He looked like a soldier, but he was not a Nazi; definitely not one of them. He was wearing a sword and a strange hat, and he was staring directly at her. She wondered whether he might be a Golem Sentinel, there to watch for any invaders, but no, the man was just a statue. She left him to his lonely vigil and looked down into the massive square below, which, to her delight, was crowded with lovely juicy people!

Heldra scampered back down the tree to observe her feast more closely. The people were all wearing big coats and woolly hats. Each one carried a mobile phone, and there was flash after flash as they pointed them first this way and that. A choir was singing nearby, and there were packed tables everywhere with people drinking, and eating food from mobile kitchens and bars. Heldra watched and waited. Metal barriers had been set up all around the base of the tree and people had draped their coats over them as they were warmed by the portable heaters. Heldra waited until no one was looking and snatched a couple of the nearest garments. Then she changed into her female form and slipped the best-fitting coat on. Suitably attired, Heldra dropped from the tree, casually vaulted the metal barriers and drifted away into the crowds.

Her mouth watered as she walked among the people. There were so many of them, and they smelled like heaven to her. Heldra crossed the road. She was shoeless, but that did not seem to draw any attention. The first tavern she reached was bright and crowded, and there were lots of people standing outside drinking. Heldra grew even more excited. She stood on the edge of the crowd for a few minutes and then went to stand next to two young men. She was confident they would soon engage with her. Heldra unzipped her new coat to show more of her best assets and made sure that she made eye contact with the taller of the two men. Her assumption was correct, and she had only been standing there for a brief time when the first man spoke to her.

"Are you waiting for someone?" said the man.

One hour later, he and Heldra were kissing and cuddling in a dark alleyway behind the construction works that were taking place around the Admiralty Arch. The restoration work had caused many of the roads leading away from Trafalgar Square to be closed, and now they were devoid of people and perfect for Heldra. The young man

The Lost Son 37

was very enthusiastic and Heldra did not hold him back. Then, just as he was close to ecstasy, Heldra pushed him away with such force that he fell backwards and smashed his head open on a piece of scaffolding.

He was shaken but still conscious. Heldra changed back to her Siren form, and the man whimpered. Heldra's body was almost reptilian; she had scaly skin and very thin limbs with bony joints. Her head was almost human in appearance, but her eyes were much wider, and her nose was cat-like – but the strangest part of her was her tail. It was the tail of a fox; red and bushy with a white tip. Heldra dropped onto all fours and bared her sharp white teeth. The man screamed but Heldra was quick and she was starving.

PC Watkins had been told by the duty sergeant that the area behind Admiralty Arch needed to be patrolled. It was party season, and there were lots of ladders and scaffolding hanging around. And as everyone knew, ladders were magnets for drunken idiots. Being a well-prepared police officer, PC Watkins had packed some nylon ties so that if he saw anything like a ladder lying around, he could make it safe.

He was just about to head over to Trafalgar Square when he heard a ripping sound and saw that some of the protective material that had been wrapped around the building had come loose. He walked over, grasped the corner of the material and pulled it tightly so that he could reattach it. But when he looked inside, he saw what he initially thought to be an enormous fox. The beast was huge, and it looked as though it was eating a mound of kebabs or half-eaten burgers. PC Watkins removed his ASP extendable baton from its pouch on his belt and gave it a flick. The fox heard him and stopped eating for a second, but it did not run away, which PC Watkins thought was strange, so he rapped the baton on the nearest exposed piece of scaffolding, and the fox turned around swiftly.

Later that evening, PC Watkins was asked to make a full report about the incident. In his report, he described how the fox-beast had bared its teeth, which were very long and thin, hissed at him, then turned and disappeared into the scaffolding. At this point, PC Watkins had called the incident in and requested backup. When it arrived in the shape of two PCs and one motorcycle-mounted police paramedic, the mound of kebabs was identified as the remains of a young man. PC Watkins returned to the Charing Cross Police Station shaken and with traces of vomit all over the front of his stab vest. After reading the report, the duty sergeant made sure that a copy was sent directly to the seventh floor and marked for the attention of DCI Judas Iscariot. Written in green biro on the front of the report were the words: *This one looks like one of yours. Sgt Henshaw.*

10

THE FORGOTTEN TREE

Sid woke up to a stone pillow and draught that ran straight through his padded coat, down his shirt front and then exited through his trouser leg. He was sleeping underneath a stone bridge – at least that is what he thought it might be. This was the second day of not knowing who he was or what he was doing. The first morning had been one of panic and fear, but he had found somewhere quiet down by the river where he could try to think and recall his own name. He had tried looking in his pockets for a wallet or some form of identification; a library card or a bus pass, perhaps. But the other rough sleepers had been there before him and his pockets were empty.

When it got dark on that first day, he had hidden himself away behind a rubbish cart down an alley, but the rats were ever curious and would not let him be. So, he had attached himself to a group of rough sleepers, hoping for safety in numbers. The experienced rough sleepers knew where to lay their weary heads and where to get food, so he was able to get a rat-free night.

Sid got up, stamped his feet to get his circulation going and then went in search of something to drink. When he returned to the spot under the bridge, he found a cat had moved in. The cat had a way of looking at him that was unnerving and he tried to move it on by waving a hand in its general direction, but the cat ignored him. Sid took things up a notch or two and unscrewed the cap off the bottle of water given to him at the church soup kitchen nearby, and was just about to squirt it at the precocious feline when the cat sat bolt upright and started talking to him.

"I wouldn't do that if I were you," said the cat.

Sid dropped the bottle of water on the ground.

"I wouldn't do that either. You'll be thirsty in five minutes and the church doesn't do refills," said the cat.

Sid looked around to see if anyone else had heard the cat speak but they were alone.

"What's your name, kid?" said the cat.

"I can't remember, sorry. And yours?" Sid replied.

"Cat Tabby, at your service," said the cat.

"It's 'Tabby Cat'," said Sid.

"No. It's not. My name is definitely Cat Tabby. What are you doing here? That snowboarding coat is worth a fortune. I'm surprised one of the other street dwellers hasn't had that off you by now," said Cat Tabby.

Sid persisted.

"It's 'Tabby Cat', like a Maine Coon cat."

"Sit down and tell me what you're doing here. Your hair and nails are in good condition, you have a full set of pearly whites in your head and you don't sound like you belong down here," said Cat Tabby.

Sid did as the cat requested and made himself comfortable amongst the empty coffee cups and fast food wrappers. Cat Tabby drew closer.

"What's your story then? Abusive parents? Absconded from one of the King's correctional facilities? Working on a documentary to get yourself a place on a film school course?" said Cat Tabby.

"I have no idea what I'm doing here, Cat Tabby. I woke up over there, underneath that bridge. I think I walked across the bridge at one point. The only other thing I can remember is being up a tree," said Sid.

"Up a tree?" said Cat Tabby.

"Something like that. My head hurts and I've got a scratch on the back of my neck that I can't explain," said Sid.

"Show me," said Cat Tabby.

Sid opened his jacket and leaned forward. Cat Tabby approached, and when he was close enough, he sniffed and inspected the scratch. The first notes of the scent hit him like a brick attached to a boxing glove and he was about to recoil but composed himself. The boy noticed the cat flinch.

"Is it septic? Has it got infected?" Sid asked.

"No. No danger of an infection. Looks like a bite though. Where were you sleeping when you got this?" said Cat Tabby.

"It wasn't last night or the night before. It's been there for a while I think," said Sid.

Cat Tabby looked closely and recognised the bite mark. But he didn't tell the boy. He wouldn't, not just yet. Cat Tabby had a nose for business and he sensed the boy might be worth a few quid to him and his partner, Dick Whittington.

"Look. Why don't you come along with me and I'll see that you get fed and you can clean yourself up. Then, we can see about finding out who you are and what you are doing down here," said Cat Tabby.

Sid looked down into Cat Tabby's golden eyes and

wondered what the hell had happened to him. He was sitting in a pile of rubbish talking to a cat.

11

THE STAR AND THE SQUARE

The Norwegian airlines flight from Oslo-Gardermoen to London Gatwick was swift and relaxing and Bosk, not usually a fan of flying, enjoyed it. The journey from Gatwick to Central London on the Gatwick Express train was not so calm. There was a hen party just returned from their soiree in Oslo in his carriage and they would not let him rest until he had performed a couple of songs for the Hen, a lovely young girl from Battersea called Natalie.

When the young women alighted from the train, Bosk followed them through the ticket gates, and when he asked Natalie where he might find the giant Norwegian Christmas Tree, she gave him directions for Trafalgar Square.

12

FOUND AND LOST

It was rare for Judas to be caught off-guard. Centuries of watching his own back and flinching at shadows had made him more sensitive to his surroundings than most. He had been called paranoid on many an occasion. He preferred to describe his constant state of alertness as 'getting his retaliation in first'. Cat Tabby was the only creature he had encountered in a long time that could surprise him.

"I'm not going to ask you how you just sauntered into New Scotland Yard, climbed seven floors and then sneaked past the security defences that Raffles the Gentleman Thief installed for the Black Museum, but I am going to ask you not to come in through the window. It's a bugger to close when it's opened from the outside," said Judas.

Cat Tabby purred then dropped from the window ledge onto the lino of Judas's office with slinky ease.

"Well met, Master of the Black Museum. How fare thee?" said Cat Tabby.

"I was having a fairly quiet day, Cat Tabby. What can I do for you?" said Judas.

The Lost Son

"No offer of a beverage? Or a tickle under the chin? Standards are slipping around here," said Cat Tabby.

"As I recall, the last person that tickled you anywhere ended up in a sewer beneath Hampton Court! And I'd offer you a coffee, but you wouldn't appreciate it," said Judas.

Cat Tabby leapt up onto Judas's desk and assumed the enigmatic bookend pose.

"I might have some information for you," he said.

"And this information? Does it come free and without obligation or am I expected to put my hand in my pocket?" said Judas.

"Nothing is free in this life! Immortality, wings, real estate. All of it comes at a price," said Cat Tabby.

"Why don't you tell me what you know and then I can put a value on it," said Judas.

Cat Tabby's tail twitched not once but twice. It was the closest thing to a card player's tell that the feline had, and Judas braced himself for the impending back and forth.

"I ran into someone recently, a boy. He's suffered some sort of amnesia and can't remember a single thing about himself. The rough sleepers on the Embankment who took him in have also taken everything he owned. He's been bitten by a Siren I think. There's an almighty whiff about him too. He's been with the Fae. I was just wondering if he might be of interest to you?" said Cat Tabby.

Judas leaned back in his leather chair and waited for the creak in the spring that denoted maximum recline. Then, he smiled and tapped his fingers on the top of the desk.

"Is the boy Fae?" Judas asked.

"No. There's not an ounce of magic in him," said Cat Tabby.

"Who or what do you think bit him?" said Judas.

"It's not one of the Serpentine lot, nor is it any of the

Sirens from Walthamstow either. This one is new, there was a coldness about her scent."

"Anything else?" said Judas.

"I think he has something to do with a tree," said Cat Tabby.

"A tree?"

"Tall green things with roots at the bottom and nests near the top."

"Very droll," said Judas.

"He stinks to high heaven of pine needles and bark," said Cat Tabby.

"Is he in danger?"

"He could be. The siren that bit him might come back and finish her meal."

"Where can I find him?" said Judas.

As soon as he said it, he regretted it.

"Well that's the thing, isn't it. I might be able to find him again, if I *really* looked, but I'm a busy cat these days and although I'd love to devote my every waking second to tracking him down and taking him somewhere safe, I do have a living to make," said Cat Tabby.

"I don't suppose you'd be able to find the time if there was a finder's fee offered?" said Judas.

"I might," said Cat Tabby.

"What do you have in mind?" said Judas.

"A silver coin, perhaps?"

"Not on all nine of your lives."

"That was a joke. I'd take a little bit of information regarding the imminent sale of the old police station in Tooting though. How much it's going for and whether there is planning permission to build a couple of flats on it."

"You and that scoundrel Dick Whittington. How much

real estate can a cat and an ex-mayor of Olde London Town need?" said Judas.

"We've got big plans, what can I say," said Cat Tabby.

"You find the boy and keep him safe for me and I'll find out what you need to know," said Judas.

"As the Master of the Black Museum commands," said Cat Tabby.

Judas sighed. He'd been outmanoeuvred by a cat – again.

"Just find him for me. And use the lift or the stairs on your way out," said Judas.

Cat Tabby did not deign to reply, he was already on his way back to the open window.

"Bloody cat," said Judas.

After the feline had slinked away Judas went to the galley kitchen at the back of the office and started to make some coffee. It was while he was grinding the coffee beans that he remembered hearing or reading something about a missing boy. There had been an Interpol report. Or was it a local thing? Judas took his cup of coffee to the window to make sure it was locked after Cat Tabby's departure, and to spend ten minutes London-watching. As he was counting the delivery angels flying hither and thither, it began to snow.

13

LITTLE DAVE

The Goulding and Ballet Christmas Party was legendary, and this year promised to be even bigger, better and messier than ever before. Their recent account win after a long drawn-out and arduous four-way pitch against some of the top advertising agencies in London had made their year-end bottom line look very healthy indeed. So, the party planning had gone up a couple of notches; no expense was spared, and many headaches were expected the following day.

Little Dave – so-called because there was another David who played rugby semi-professionally at the weekends and was a half-giant, half-Northern man from the agency's creative department – had been drinking milk and eating sausage rolls since dawn because he was a lightweight and didn't want to expire before the Christmas party had even started, as he had done the year before. He wanted to try to chat up the new television producer during the party and, on the advice of a friend, had consumed close to four litres of semi-skimmed. But it had not quite done the trick, and he was feeling a little light-headed as the creative department warmed up for the party with a few beers at their local drinking establishment, the Charing Cross Scepter.

Little Dave looked around the pub and realised that his vision had already started to blur, and he decided that now was a good time to slip away. He bought his round first, of course. He didn't need any of the others teasing him about having short arms and long pockets again. Then he pretended to go to the toilet and branched off for the exit before anyone noticed. Once clear of the pub, he wandered down St Martin's Lane to Trafalgar Square, where he would grab a seat in front of the National Portrait Gallery and sober up a little. Little Dave was from Sunderland, and he was always ready to tell anyone within earshot that he was a Northerner. The truth was quite the opposite though. Little Dave loved London and he couldn't really imagine going back to the North East. All he needed to make his life perfect was a girlfriend.

Heldra saw the little man zig-zag through the crowds, clearly under the influence of drink, and perch on the stone steps behind the Christmas Tree. He was perfect. He was slight and easy to carry, and he looked lonely. She unbuttoned her blouse to show plenty of cleavage and sat down next to him.

"I love this time of year, don't you?" she said.

Little Dave sat upright and ran his fingers through his hair. He wasn't used to female interaction, and the attentions of this beautiful red-headed woman surprised him.

"Yes, who doesn't?" said Little Dave.

Heldra almost giggled at the boy's eagerness.

"Some people don't like company at this time of year. They prefer to be alone and see all this warmth, happiness and joy as being a bit false," said Heldra.

"Humbug!" said Little Dave.

"Humbug? I don't think I understand. I'm from Norway. Can you explain?" said Heldra.

Little Dave was not used to small talk, and he'd always found it a bit difficult, but this beautiful, well-endowed woman seemed keen on him.

"Humbug. Like in *A Christmas Carol*. Ebeneezer Scrooge says it a lot at the beginning. When he wants to crush people's joy. Have you read the book or seen any of the films?" said Little Dave.

"I must have at some point, but I forget. I'd love it if you could remind me of the story over a beer perhaps?" said Heldra.

Little Dave became remarkably sober.

"There's a pub I know, not far from here. It's quiet, and I can buy you that beer and tell you all about the ghosts of Christmas Past, Present and Future," said Little Dave.

Heldra could see that the boy was getting excited.

"I'd love to. What's your name?" she said.

"Dave. And you are?"

"Heldra, nice to meet you, Dave," said Heldra.

Little Dave stood up and almost wet himself when the beautiful woman took his hand in hers. They walked across the square to the top of the Mall, and Little Dave pointed to the Silver Cross pub.

"It's normally quiet. The landlord doesn't like tourists. He prefers the custom of the secret sorts that work over there in the Admiralty Arch," said Little Dave.

"You know this area really well, don't you," said Heldra.

The boy's chest puffed up with pride, and he escorted her across the road and into the pub. Heldra saw the look on his face and smiled, but she chided herself for being too obvious. The little man was a little drunk, but she needed to be far more careful than she had been so far. Once inside and seated at a small table at the back of the pub, Little Dave excused himself and went to the bar. He returned to the table with two large tankards of mulled wine. The Silver Cross was a normal boozer, very happy to serve the basics and serve them well. They didn't normally go in for fripperies and seasonal nonsense, but mulled wine was their Christmas special. It came in old-fashioned pewter tankards, and Little Dave knew that the Norwegian girl would love them.

"If we're going to talk about Christmas and Scrooge and all things Humbug, we need to be drinking one of these," said Little Dave.

Heldra thanked Little Dave and warmed her hands on her tankard. Little Dave was clearly pleased with his choice of venue and beverage. The woman sitting opposite really seemed to be into him, and he was feeling great. His phone started to vibrate with text messages from his friends at the agency. He imagined they were all wondering where he was, but he did not care. The girl from television could wait; he was on to a good thing.

Heldra watched the boy and could see the anticipation in his eyes. He was already undressing her in his mind and trying to work out when or if he should suggest that they find somewhere quiet where they could be alone. He made his move shortly after.

"I'm expected at a party later but I'd rather talk to you to be honest. I don't know what your plans are?" said Little Dave.

"I don't want to make you miss your party but I am enjoying talking to you," said Heldra.

Little Dave did not really have a decision to make; he'd swerve that party in a heartbeat if he was given half the chance to take things further with Heldra.

"It's not that important, to be honest. We could get something to eat if you want?" said Little Dave.

"That sounds perfect to me. I'm absolutely starving," said Heldra. They ate at the nearby Pizza Express. Halfway through the Doppio dough balls, Heldra whispered to Little Dave.

"After we've finished this, we should go somewhere with a bed. I like to lie down after a meal."

Little Dave wolfed down his New York Hottest like a man possessed. He was already visualising what he would do with Heldra. When the waitress came to give them the bill, Little Dave surprised her with a fifty-pound note and told her to keep the change. They checked in to the Trafalgar Hotel at 14.00hrs.

DCI Judas Iscariot was called at 15.00hrs by the duty sergeant at Scotland Yard and told that a 'Black Museum' sort of incident had just taken place. A young man had been attacked in a hotel room on St Martin's Lane. He had been savaged and bitten quite badly. There appeared to have been a scuffle, and one of the hotel windows had been shattered. The management called the Police. When the attending officers entered the room, at 14.30hrs, they saw a woman wearing a costume. She appeared to be dressed as a big cat, a snow leopard perhaps, and she was on top of a man licking blood from a wound on his shoulder. When the officers challenged the woman dressed as the snow leopard, she attempted to bite them and then leapt through the open window and disappeared. The ambulance arrived at 14.45hrs, and the man was taken to hospital. The paramedics reported that he was hysterical and was eventually sedated. He was admitted to hospital, his wounds were dressed, and he was now in a private room with a police officer in attendance.

Judas thanked the duty sergeant for informing him. He told him that he would head straight over to the hospital and that no one should talk to the patient before he did. Then he called a Shaper named Sebastian Wonglehurst who did occasional work for the Black Museum.

"Sebastian," said Judas.

"Inspector," replied Sebastian Wonglehurst.

The Shaper was in a bar by the sounds of it and Judas inwardly groaned.

"I need you to come and help me with something. Are you compos mentis, Sebastian?" said Judas.

"As compos as the next magical creature, probably even more so," said Sebastian.

"You had better be. Meet me at the Charing Cross Hospital. Now," said Judas.

"I shall be there in the squeezing of a lemon. Am I bringing my easel? Or is this just another copycat gig?" Sebastian enquired.

"Bring your pad and pencils please," said Judas.

Sebastian was not entirely sober when he arrived at the hospital, but he was bright and bushy tailed. Wonglehurst was Fae. His mother had been a Shaper, a creature that can take on the form of any other magical being as long as they have seen it once before, and his father had been a forger, so he could not only draw what others saw but could then imitate them. Judas had used Sebastian on a few sting operations where Sebastian had pretended to be a potential victim. He was a talented actor, and brave.

Judas briefed him outside the door to Little Dave's room.

"Sebastian, thanks for coming at such short notice. I hope I haven't dragged you away from anything important?" said Judas.

"A couple of City boys have been buying me champagne

all day. They think I'm some sort of Gordon Gecko type," said Sebastian.

"You're okay to do this?" said Judas.

"Inspector, please!" said Sebastian.

He pretended to be offended and fluttered his lashes at Judas.

"The man behind this door is Plain Folk. I think he's been attacked by one of yours, Fae I mean, and I want to know what this creature is and why it's attacking one of them. The Underworld beneath the London Underground knows that the Plain Folk are off limits, so whatever this is, they aren't from these parts. Once you get a good likeness with your pencils, show him the drawing and then if he's still a little confused, turn into whatever you've drawn and we'll get a proper idea," said Judas.

"Child's play," said Sebastian.

Judas tapped on the door and entered, followed by Sebastian Wonglehurst the artist.

Judas excused the police constable who was keeping an eye on Little Dave and pulled up a chair so that he could talk with him.

"Can you hear me?" said Judas.

Little Dave was lying flat on his back and covered in bandages from his waist upwards to the base of his chin. He was on a drip and wired for sound. He looked in a bad way and Judas wasn't sure that he'd be able to get much from him.

"Is it David or Dave?" said Judas.

"He looks like a Dave," said Sebastian.

"Pipe down. You concentrate on getting a good likeness if our man here is able to describe his attacker," said Judas.

"Dave. I go by Dave."

Little Dave could hardly talk, and his voice came out in a hoarse whisper.

"Dave. Hello. I'm from the Met, and this is our resident artist. With your help he's going to draw the person who attacked you," said Judas.

Little Dave shuddered at the mention of his attacker and whimpered as the slight movement caused him pain.

"Can you describe this person?" said Judas.

"Not a person. She's a monster," said Little Dave.

Judas knew well enough that he did not need to play any games with the wounded man in the bed in front of him, all he needed do was let him ramble and Sebastian would do the rest.

"She was a little taller than me, with red hair and nice large...eyes. I thought she liked me and we checked into a hotel. Then, she took her clothes off, and we got on the bed," said Little Dave.

"The constable and the paramedic have already told us what you told them, Dave. Can you just describe what she looked like before she attacked you, and then what she turned into, please?" said Judas.

Sebastian let out a little groan.

"That was just getting good, Inspector. Shame on you," he said.

Little Dave shifted in his bed and grimaced. He was clearly in pain.

"She was buxom and healthy in that Scandinavian way. Red hair, long and shiny. Then she grew a tail; a fox tail! It was swishing around and I couldn't take my eyes off it. Then she looked at me and her mouth split wide open to reveal a load of sharp teeth. I'm talking about rows and rows of the bloody things. I freaked out, but she just gurgled and snarled. I remember her body going a grey colour and it moved like it was an accordion, just before you pull the thing open. Big gaps appeared between her ribs like she was being stretched," said Little Dave.

Sebastian's pencil was moving at great speed now, scratching and shading the paper, forming a shape and adding extra bits.

"Then she bit me!" shrieked Little Dave.

Judas could see that they were about to lose Little Dave to the warm embrace of another round of painkillers.

"Sebastian. Show him the picture," Judas ordered.

Little Dave peered at the drawing and flinched. But it was not enough for Judas. He needed to be absolutely sure what had attacked the young man in the bed.

"Sebastian, put the pad and the pencil down and show Little Dave the 3D version," said Judas.

Sebastian stood up and took a quick look around the hospital room for cameras. Then, he blinked twice and turned into the beast that Little Dave had been describing. Little Dave screamed and then passed out. Sebastian changed back into his human form and Judas hit the panic button on the wall behind Little Dave's bed.

"Well, that was rather conclusive," said Judas.

"You could say that. What the hell is a Woodland Siren doing in the middle of London at Christmas?" said Sebastian.

"Keep that to yourself or I'll be putting you in the Black Museum until the New Year. I don't want anyone panicking, let alone any other Sirens hunting for this one. I know how territorial they get," said Judas.

The two of them left Little Dave in the capable hands of the nurses and departed. Judas thanked Sebastian, and the Shaper wandered off to find another bar where he could encourage some inebriated City boys to buy him more champagne. As Sebastian drifted away into the crowd, more snowflakes began to fall. Judas returned to Scotland Yard and handed the drawing of Heldra in her human form to Sergeant Henshaw, asking that her image be copied and circulated to all officers. She was a person of interest to the Black Museum and the Met, and she was to be approached with all caution because she was dangerous when cornered.

14

WIPPER AND WASP

Bosk had been playing for an hour and had drawn a good crowd. His case was open at his feet, and it was already half full of coins of varying weights and colours: some kind soul had even dropped a crisp five-pound note in it for him. Bosk played on; he was mixing his music up, introducing a ditty here and there that he knew would attract some of his own kind, as well as a tune or two for the Plain Folk. He noticed a cat sitting nonchalantly on top of a plinth. It kept giving him strange looks, and he wondered if his disguise was slipping.

Bosk stopped playing. The crowd had swelled, and he had already made eye contact with one gnome and two sprites. He felt sure they would be able to help him. People drifted away and as Bosk was scooping up a handful of coins from his case, one of the sprites approached.

"Well met, brother," said the sprite.

"Well met indeed. My name is Bosk."

"You have a way with that fiddle," said the sprite.

"I muddle along," said Bosk. "And you are?"

"Wipper, and that handsome chap over there is my brother Wasp," said Wipper.

Bosk looked up to see that Wasp was already working the crowd.

"He will only take a few pennies, brother Bosk. It is the Festive Season, after all," said Wipper.

"I'm glad to hear it," said Bosk.

Wasp ambled over and tugged at an imaginary forelock.

"That was fine playing, some real pretty finger work," said Wasp.

"You are too kind. I wonder, could you help me with something?" said Bosk.

"If we can, we will. If not, we'll try and point you in the right direction of someone or something that might," said Wipper.

Bosk placed the five-pound note into Wasp's hand and then finished pocketing his earnings.

"An advance," said Bosk.

The note disappeared before his eyes.

"A young lad, he'll be in his teens, was taken from his parents in Oslo. I have decided to help return him to his kin. Have you heard of such a boy?" said Bosk.

Wasp leaned across to his brother and whispered something in his ear. Wipper shrugged and then nodded.

"There was a boy who turned up no more than a week ago. A strange one. He has lost his memory or something. He was fleeced by the other rough sleepers of course. They had his gold away before he was even awake but left him his clothes, so not all bad," said Wipper.

"He could be anyone, a runaway. What makes you think he might be the boy from Oslo?" said Bosk.

"He came when the tree came," said Wasp.

"And he smelled just like it," said Wipper.

Bosk placed his fiddle inside his case and slung it over his shoulder.

"And there was the other thing," said Wasp.

"What other thing?" said Bosk.

"There have been two attacks on the Plain Folk hereabouts. The rumour is that a Siren has started to hunt here," said Wipper.

Bosk didn't need to ask who the Siren was.

"Where can I find the boy?" he enquired.

"Down by the river. They call it the South Bank," said Wasp.

"Thank you both. If you ever come to Oslo, ask for me. I should be glad to repay the favour," said Bosk.

Wasp and his brother Wipper gave Bosk a sort of lazy salute and then turned away and disappeared into what was left of the crowd. Bosk looked at the huge Christmas tree in the square. Heldra would return to it at some point. He just needed to find the boy, sing him a song that would give him back his memory, and then deal with Heldra. He was just about to go in search of the South Bank when the cat from the plinth appeared.

"Good afternoon," said the cat.

Bosk looked down.

"It is still afternoon, is it not? We may have strayed into early evening," the cat added.

"I thought you had the look of the Fae about you," said Bosk.

"And you are not just a busker, are you," said Cat Tabby.

"I am known as Bosk, and you are?"

"My name is Cat Tabby, a friend of this fine city."

"Well met, Cat Tabby," said Bosk.

The cat jumped up onto one of the plastic picnic-style tables and looked at Bosk. His tailed swished from left to right, and Bosk sensed that the cat might be trying to read his thoughts.

"I hope you don't think I'm being rude, Bosk, but I did overhear what you were talking about with your friends just now. I think I may be able to help you to find the boy," said Cat Tabby.

Bosk did not entirely trust the feline. There was something about it he could not put his finger on, but he needed as much information as he could get – the boy must be found, after all.

"Do you know of him or his whereabouts?" Bosk asked.

"Not precisely, I'm afraid. What I can tell you is that there is a nasty piece of work that wants the boy found and if they get there first, the boy might not survive the meeting," said Cat Tabby.

"The Siren?" said Bosk.

"No, not the Siren. This creature's name is Judas Iscariot," said Cat Tabby.

"And why does this Judas Iscariot want the boy?" said Bosk.

"I try not to think about that," said Cat Tabby.

Bosk gripped the strap of his fiddle case. He knew that he might have to fight Heldra, but now it appeared that there was another hurdle in his way.

"I know that I haven't been able to help much in finding the boy but I think I might be able to help in another way," said Cat Tabby.

"And what might that be?"

"I know where Judas lives, and I know that he'll be going there later on tonight. I can take you there if you like?"

"How much?" said Bosk.

"Nothing, my friend. Think of it as a good deed," said Cat Tabby.

Bosk looked into those green eyes and knew that this cat had never done a good deed in its life from which it had not profited. But he was a stranger in this town, and he decided to take a gamble.

"Lead on then, Cat Tabby," said Bosk.

The cat tiptoed its way through the crowds until it reached the road. Bosk was stunned when he saw it place a paw to its mouth and produce a piercing whistle.

"Taxi!" shouted Cat Tabby.

A black Hackney Cab swerved across the road, narrowly missing a rickshaw transporting three women dressed for a party, and pulled up at the kerb. The door to the cab swung open, and Cat Tabby casually jumped in. Bosk followed and found that the cat was already sitting comfortably on the seat with its seatbelt in place.

"Little Venice please, driver," said Cat Tabby.

Bosk settled back, and the cab pulled away. They were only halfway up St Martin's Lane when Cat Tabby started to give Bosk the guided tour.

"On the left is the National Portrait Gallery, and over there..."

15

A FACE IN THE CROWD

Heldra was in hiding. She had run in blind panic from the hotel room after the police had surprised her. At first, she had sought her means of escape by climbing up and then running along the tops of the buildings, but then the buildings stopped. She found that she could not go any further in that direction, and then she saw an open space in front of her, with trees and a lake, and she ran for it. At first, she hid in the bushes, but there was no way that she could stay there in daylight without being discovered. So, she crept as quietly as she could to the water's edge and lowered herself in. The water was shallow and was only just deep enough to cover her head, but at least she was safe there – for now.

As she waited for the park to empty, Heldra thought back to the hotel room, and her stomach grumbled. The police had surprised her, and she had been forced to flee, and now, because she was unfamiliar with the city, she had run away from the square where her tree was located. Heldra was angry with herself and hissed loudly. The sudden and unexpected outburst frightened a few of the ducks that were going about their own business nearby, and they quacked loudly, which caused the geese to honk.

The water was warm and inviting compared to the lakes and the rivers of her homeland, and she would have been able to stay in it for as long as she wanted to, but she had injured herself when she had jumped through the window, and now she had a flesh wound to go with her wounded pride. Heldra raised her head from the water and looked around. Nearby was a small island and on it was a little cottage. There were no lights on in the window so Heldra swam towards it. There were lots of long, thick reeds and marsh grasses at the edge of the island, and she was able to slither through them and creep into a woodshed behind the cottage. It was dry inside, but the ground was an inch deep in duck and goose faeces, and Heldra almost hissed again but held her nose and stayed silent.

The noise of the people in the park and the cars and buses on the roads finally died away, and Heldra decided she would risk moving. She made her way back to the water, slipped in, and swam away from the cottage, knowing that the filth of the woodshed would be washed away and that when she exited the water, she would no longer smell like rotten flesh. Heldra reached a bridge across the lake and waited beneath it. Then, when she believed the coast was clear, she reached up and grasped the edge of the metal bridge, and with one powerful heave, she pulled herself from the lake. There was no one in sight, and she sprinted for the nearest tree, hid behind it, and then transformed back into her human form. If she was lucky, and if she stayed in the shadows, she might get back to the square, her tree, and safety.

Heldra soon discovered that she was not as far from her lair as she had thought. In fact, she was only a few hundred feet away. The great Arch that she had lured the boy to was directly in front of her, and no more than a stone's throw from the Arch was the column with the little man with one arm. Next to that was her tree. She started to run for it but saw something then that caused her to stop in her tracks. There was a piece of paper pasted onto a wall, and on it was her face, her human face! The police knew what she looked like now, but it did not appear that they knew what she was – not yet. Heldra raced for the tree then and clambered up its branches until she reached her place of safety, where she curled up into a ball and slept. In the morning, she would make a plan to escape.

16

OUT OF TUNE

Judas had moved to Little Venice shortly after his flat in East London had received a visit from Lucifer, the Morningstar. The Devil left an unwelcome imprint on everything he touched and the flat had ceased to feel like home to Judas, and more of a reminder of the darker aspects of life. So, he went west and found a charming little narrowboat called *Rosie*. She was your archetypal canal-going vessel, long and narrow, but she had been looked after by the Water Sprites that lived in Little Venice and was surprisingly roomy.

He had already stopped at the *little Waitrose in Paddington Station and picked up some food and two bottles of Chilean red, and was looking forward to a quiet night, when the scar – the one that ran from his belly button all the way up his stomach to his breastbone – started to burn. The scar was his early warning system and throbbed when danger was near, but Judas could see no one on the towpath, either in front of him or behind. It was completely empty. Judas placed his bag of shopping down on the ground very gently. He had purchased some shiitake mushrooms and free-range eggs and didn't want to be making an omelette out of them. When he straightened up, there was a busker standing in front of him with some sort of musical instrument in a case slung over one shoulder.

"Evening," said the busker.

"Evening," said Judas.

"Fancy a song, Inspector?"

"Do I have a choice?" said Judas.

"Not really," said the busker.

Judas saw the busker's mouth open and seconds later he felt as though he'd been punched in the chest by an East End Golem.

When he woke up, he was sitting on the roof of the narrowboat with his hands tied behind his back. The iron chain that Judas normally used to secure *Rosie* to the towpath when the weather took a turn for the worse was wound around his legs and the other end was attached to his spare generator. Needless to say, the generator was perched on the side of the narrowboat, ready to be pushed overboard if the busker did not get what he wanted.

"Oh, you're awake. Good," said a voice from behind him.

Judas gave the chains a quick kick to see how tight they were and then groaned. Whoever the busker was, he had done this sort of thing before.

"I'm a police officer you know," said Judas.

"I was told you would say that," said the voice.

Judas sighed.

"This isn't going to end well for you, let me tell you. Why don't you show yourself and we can talk about whatever is bothering you?" said Judas.

He heard shuffling and then sensed movement.

"Here I am."

Judas looked up. The busker was no more, and in his

place was a rangy Woodland Sprite with long dark hair and piercing blue eyes. Its limbs were thin, but they looked strong and the sprite was obviously very capable.

"*Rosie*, or should I say this narrowboat, was rented to me by one of your kin. In fact, he lives over there on that small island with the big willow tree on it. Have you called in to say hello yet?" said Judas.

The sprite looked up quickly and stared back down the canal towards the island with the willow tree. Sprites are very territorial and can turn nasty if formalities are not observed.

"You haven't checked in, have you," said Judas.

The sprite looked perturbed and started to hum to itself. It was a sad tune, and Judas deduced the sprite was conjuring some sort of spell. The sprite stopped abruptly and looked back down at Judas.

"That should do it for now. It's not one of my best but it should keep my brothers and sisters from discovering me for a little while longer."

"What's your name?" said Judas.

"I am Bosk," said the sprite.

"Nice to meet you, Bosk. Now, why are you here and what do you want from me?" said Judas.

"I'm reliably informed that you are searching for a young man, recently arrived from Norway," said Bosk.

"That is a police matter, Bosk."

"Of course. I'm also told that you make a lot of money from rescuing poor lost cases like this boy, and then charging those looking for them for their return," said Bosk.

"Whoever told you that is a liar, Bosk," said Judas.

"I'm sure they are, but I have no one else to trust right now and I need to reach the boy before something happens to him," said Bosk.

"And does this something have long red hair, long talons and rows of sharp teeth?" said Judas.

"You've met Heldra it seems," said Bosk.

"Not exactly, but I do have a name for her now, thank you," said Judas.

The Woodland Sprite appeared agitated and Judas guessed its spell might be weakening and it needed to move fast. Judas watched as the sprite reached in the case it was carrying and took out a fiddle and a bow. Then it started to play, and Judas felt a blade being drawn across his chest and blood flowing down his torso. Each time Bosk drew the bow backwards, the knife cut into Judas's flesh.

"Where is the boy?" said Bosk.

"I have no idea," said Judas.

"I have a large number of songs and tunes to play, murderer," said Bosk.

"I have been cursed by God, sprite. I cannot die. You can sing all you want and I might pass out, but you'll get nothing from me, and now that I've seen your face and know what you are, there will be nowhere that you can hide from me, not in this city anyway," said Judas.

"Where is the boy?" said Bosk.

He was still playing but his voice had dropped. Either he was angry or frustrated.

"If you don't tell me where the boy is, his blood will be on your hands. The Siren will find him eventually, and she will not spare him," said Bosk.

"I don't know where he is," said Judas.

"Well, you give me no choice," said Bosk.

Judas watched as the sprite put its precious fiddle and bow away and then nonchalantly gave the chains a nudge with the side of one long bony foot. Judas heard them rattle and then splash as they hit the surface of the water. Then, he watched as the generator, his beautiful new generator, wobbled and then disappeared over the side. He felt an almighty pull and then he was flying across the deck and into the rancid dark water of the canal. He had been planning on a quiet night in with some decent food and a glass or two of wine but instead, he had been tortured by a sprite with a fiddle and then left to drown.

'Bloody wonderful' he thought as he hit the bottom of the canal.

Bosk jumped down from the narrowboat and walked down the towpath towards the big station and the tall buildings. He needed to get away from Little Venice quickly. The resident sprites that lived there would not take kindly to him wandering hither and thither without their consent. As he walked away, he could not help but feel that there was something not quite right about the situation. The cat had described the man that he had just sent to the bottom of the canal as a cold-blooded murderer, but Bosk had not seen that in the man at all. When he met with the cat later, he would get to the bottom of it.

17

OXLEAS

Sid still could not remember his own name, and although by nature he was the stoic sort, he was chastising himself. Knowing one's own name was paramount to knowing what sort of person one was and where one came from. He had tried a few names on already. Was he a Gary? Or a Quentin? Maybe he was a Stewart? Or a Martin? None of them seemed quite right, which he was strangely happy about. He had decided to trust his instincts. If he didn't feel like a Gary, then he probably wasn't.

There was another cause for his burgeoning anger, and it was padding alongside him on four soft paws. The talking cat wouldn't stop talking, and it was beginning to grate on him. He had pictured himself giving the chatty little feline a quick punt into the hedgerow more than once in the last hour but had controlled himself. Apart from the cat, he knew no one.

"Do you know anything about Oxleas Woodlands?" Cat Tabby asked.

"No. Possibly. I might! You know, once my memory comes back, I might know all about it," said Sid.

"Quite. Well, Oxleas is thousands of years old. Spirits, elves, gnomes and all sorts of other creatures lived in these woods. The men and women came along much later and started chopping down the trees to make the ships that would go on to defeat the Spanish and French navies. The bark from the trees was used to dye the leathers and the skins to make clothes and the charcoal went into everything else. Then, the Industrial Revolution came along, and everything changed. These woods used to cover thousands of hectares, and I've traipsed across most of them," said Cat Tabby.

"You're telling me that you are thousands of years old then?" said Sid.

"That and more. Oh yes! I've been around since the very beginning," said Cat Tabby.

"May I ask why we're going back in time then?" said Sid.

"We're not more than a hop-skip-and-a-jump from the Thames here. Plus, there are lots of places to hide, and you'll be able to rest here while I find out who you really are, where you are from, and how to get you back there," said Cat Tabby.

He hadn't mentioned the fact that he was planning on hyping up the reward for the boy and that he was already playing the sprite with the fiddle and his old friend Judas off against each other. Cat Tabby was a complex creature. He was capable of magnificent feats of bravery and daring one minute, and then the next, he could smile and swish his tail about while standing by and watching bloody murder being done. But the boy didn't need to know that.

They reached a narrow path that led into the forest. It was a strange sensation because here, under the canopy of branches and leaves, they were most definitely in the woods, but the sounds of London were ever present. They could hear the planes passing overhead on their way to London City Airport, the sirens from the ambulances and the police cars roaring up and down the A207, Shooter's Hill, and the trains snorting and grunting their way out of the station at Falconwood to the south.

Cat Tabby led Sid down the path, and after a couple of lefts and rights, they emerged into a clearing. On the far side of it was a VW Campervan. Cat Tabby padded across the grass and as he reached the van, the side door slid open. Sid's mouth opened with it. Inside the van was a boudoir. It couldn't be anything else. There appeared to be miles of silk wrapped around everything in sight. Cushions, curtains and tables were all purple and silky.

"You'll be fine here. I'll be back shortly. Eat what you find and maybe take a bath; you're beginning to kick up a bit," said Cat Tabby.

Sid raised an arm above his head and was greeted with an unwelcome and highly potent waft of something unpleasant.

"That's what friends are for," said Cat Tabby.

Sid didn't remember ever asking to be the cat's friend but stepped inside the VW and went in search of a bathroom. Cat Tabby touched the sliding door with his paw and watched as it shut, and he heard it lock. Then, he turned around and set off for London. If his cunning plan was going to plan, Judas would have been roughed up a bit and thankful for any help that Cat Tabby might give him; the sprite Bosk would think that Cat Tabby was trustworthy; and the boy, God bless him, would help him get a tidy sum from the parents. All-in-all, it had been a good couple of days.

18

THE RIGHT SPRITE

Judas had been in the water for just over an hour when the Paddington Basin Water Sprites discovered him. He had been trying in vain to shake off the chains that bound him to the generator, so was more than pleased to see a pair of luminous eyes approaching. The Water Sprite had not been looking for him, merely going about its business, and seeing Judas sitting there chained to a brand-new generator gave him a shock. He disappeared quickly and returned with some help. After they had pulled him out of the water and he had vomited most of the canal back up and onto the towpath, he was able to tell them all about his recent guest. The sprites listened intently, growing increasingly angry as he retold his tale. The leader of the Water Sprites, who was Judas's de facto landlord, whispered to two of his lads and they raced away. Judas presumed that they were going in search of the trespasser.

He thanked the Water Sprites for saving him and they asked if he needed anything else. Judas took them up on their kind offer and asked them to pick up some more eggs, some fresh shiitake mushrooms and at least three bottles of Chilean red. He had imbibed far too much of the Paddington Basin brown and needed to cleanse his palette. Then he went inside *Rosie*, took a long, hot shower, and waited for the ingredients to arrive.

Bosk would not get far; he had a pack of angry Water Sprites on his tail now. Judas was feeling a touch irate about the assault and wanted his pound of sprite flesh for ruining his Kilgour two-piece suit and his brand-new Loakes. There was also the issue of the identity of the soon-to-be arrested idiot who had given the sprite his name and suggested that he might be a bent copper.

Judas heard the knock on the galley door, and when he opened it, he found that the Water Sprites had delivered not three but four bottles of Concha Y Toro Don Melchor, a very fine Cabernet Sauvignon from the Maipo Valley, and a basket of very fresh shiitake mushrooms.

19

THE CAT TRAP

Cat Tabby arrived in Trafalgar Square at the height of the rush hour. The traffic was doing some bizarre form of metal conga dance. The cars and buses were bumper to bumper, and when the music of the pedestrian crossings started and the red lights changed from red to flashing amber to green, they all moved forward a foot or two and then came to a halt. Cat Tabby imagined all the drivers sticking an arm out of their respective windows and shouting 'Hey!' as they moved.

"Let's all do the conga, let's all do the traffic jam," Cat Tabby sang to himself as he slipped through the legs of the tourists and the commuters.

He had decided that the Christmas tree in the square was worth looking at more closely. The boy smelled of the tree. The boy remembered something about the tree. He had a connection to the tree. Maybe the boy had left some clue about his family or home in the tree? Cat Tabby slipped under the protective iron railings between any revellers and the base of the tree, jumped up on one of the huge chains that anchored it to the ground, and ran up it with feline ease, disappearing amongst the branches.

The noise of the world outside ceased as soon as Cat Tabby reached the trunk of the tree, and he froze. There was something not quite right, and his back arched and eyes widened. He started to climb, and his sense of unease grew the higher he went. Cat Tabby was nearly at the top when he caught a scent in the air. It was like a woman's perfume mixed with something pungent, and he realised too late that he knew that smell well. It was fresh, bloody meat.

Heldra heard the cat creeping among the branches of her tree, slipped out of her hiding place, and waited for it on a sturdy branch. The cat came closer and closer until it was within striking range. Then she snatched it up and took it into her darkness. There was not much meat on the thing, but it would do for now.

Cat Tabby felt the sharp talons close around his throat, and he knew instantly that if he struggled and fought back, the beast would snap his neck before he had a chance to talk his way out of his current predicament. So, he waited until the beast stopped moving and was about to open its mouth.

Heldra placed the little cat down on the crushed branches she had used to make her secret platform at the top of the tree and prepared to bite its head off. But, just as she was about to sink her teeth into the cat's neck, it spoke to her.

"I wouldn't do that if I were you. I have news for you. And a proposition," said Cat Tabby hurriedly.

Heldra snarled and drew back.

"Thank you," said Cat Tabby. "I believe you are looking for a young lad from Oslo?"

"I was looking for him a while ago, and if that's your

news my scrawny little friend, you're going to be working your way through my gut in five minutes," said Heldra.

Cat Tabby tried to stand up, but the beast held him down.

"I hear you are also on the run. The Black Museum is after you, Siren. I can get you out of the city and back home without them knowing," said Cat Tabby.

Heldra released the cat and sat up. She was monstrous in the small space, and her scent was even more powerful. It made Cat Tabby's eyes water.

"So, that's your proposition is it? I spare you, and you give me the boy and arrange to spirit me away and across the sea to Norway?" said Heldra.

"There is also the small matter of the creature that is hunting you. The Woodland Sprite. He calls himself Bosk. Do you know him?" said Cat Tabby.

Heldra hissed, and Cat Tabby gulped.

"He's here?" said Heldra.

Cat Tabby noticed that the tone of her voice had changed. She was not afraid of Bosk, but she was certainly wary of him.

"Yes. He's around somewhere. I can let you know where he is, or I could let him know where you are if you want to ambush him," said Cat Tabby.

Heldra growled and stroked one of Cat Tabby's ears with one razor-sharp talon.

"You're a cunning little one. What is your name?" said Heldra.

"Cat Tabby. And you are?"

"I am the Siren, Heldra," she said.

"Nice to meet you. Now, I have an offer to make. I can give you Bosk, and I can get you out of town. In exchange, I want the boy; he's worth a lot of reward money to me. Deal?" said Cat Tabby.

Heldra purred. It sounded like a mini-chainsaw, and Cat Tabby thought for one horrible moment that he could see her rows of sharp teeth moving backwards and forwards just like the teeth on a real chainsaw. But she was just laughing.

"How are you going to get me out of the city and back home?" said Heldra.

"You leave that to me. I have friends in the Mayor's Office, and there are plenty of ships that run up and down this river that will turn a blind eye to another box or crate on the deck," said Cat Tabby.

"When?" said Heldra.

"Well, it's like this. Your friend Bosk wants to steal my reward, so I need you to get rid of him for me. Once the sprite is no more, I'll have you on the next boat that passes the Embankment," said Cat Tabby.

"Okay. Where is Bosk?" said Heldra.

"Leave that to me too. I'll bring him here, and you can take care of him," said Cat Tabby.

"I like you, my devious little friend. Have you ever laid with a Siren?" said Heldra.

"I wish I had the time, fair Heldra. But I must be on my way," said Cat Tabby.

He heard Heldra snorting with laughter as he almost fell down the entire length of the tree in his haste to get away from her.

20

MARMITE

Sid bathed until his fingertips turned the colour of compacted snow, and he dropped off twice and woke up with a snort as the bathwater entered his nostrils. He got up and put his clothes back on, then found some bread and a fresh unopened jar of Marmite. He feasted on the yeast extract, and in between bites, he wondered who had left the jar in this odd boudoir inside a VW Campervan in a forest clearing in the middle of London.

Sid grew thoughtful and sat back on one of the giant purple pillows. It was perhaps due to the taste of the Marmite that he started to see faces. Not magical floating faces, but the faces of a man and a woman and then the faces of people he judged to be the same age as he was. His memory was starting to come back to him, and for the first time in what felt like months, Sid felt happier and less muddled.

He finished the Marmite and went in search of a bin for the empty jar. He felt a little guilty when the thick brown glass jar with its bright yellow lid hit the bottom of the plastic bin with a hearty but reassuring thud, but then something occurred to him. He needed to get back to the tree as soon as possible! It was the first thing he had remembered, and he felt it was probably the best place to start looking for answers to his loss of memory.

Sid left the boudoir in the same state he had found it and went to the door. He grasped the handle and gave it a pull, but the door did not budge. He tried again and then again, but the result remained the same.

"That bloody cat!" Sid cried.

But Sid was a calm sort, and he was determined to find a solution to his predicament. Part of him wanted to find a heavy object and hurl it through a window, but that would be hasty and altogether brutish. Sid looked around the campervan. There were a few small windows above the sliding door, but that was it. The wheel and windscreen were missing from the front of the van, replaced by long drapes and wall hangings. But then, Sid looked up, and he saw that the VW Campervan had a false roof that extended upwards like a concertina. The concertina was made of fabric, silk by the look of it, and all Sid needed to cut through it was a sharp object. A piece of heavy brown glass should do it.

Sid left the strange Campervan and the little forest in the middle of the city and retraced his steps until he came to a road called Shooter's Hill. The centre of the city was clearly signposted, and Sid set off in that direction. A big lorry passed him by, and he felt something hit his leg. It was a piece of grit, and when he looked at the rear of the lorry, there was a sign on it warning everyone to take care. 'Heavy snow' was coming. Sid snuffled into the collar of his snowboarding jacket. This wasn't snow, he knew that much.

21

ALL ROADS LEAD TO TRAFALGAR

Judas woke up without a sore head even though he had demolished all four bottles of the magnificent Chilean red the Water Sprites had left him. The evidence of his vino-gluttony was to be found in the galley kitchen, alongside a plate that had been wiped clean and very possibly licked. After God had cursed him with immortality and then cast him out, Judas discovered that although he could not be killed, he could be harmed. Another one of God's little jokes. But mercifully, hangovers had not been included in his curse.

He dressed in a sharp Paul Smith two-piece and a pair of the maestro's own shoes. His new Loakes were still drying in the galley. He wondered if they would ever recover. Judas brewed some coffee, drank it on the upper deck, and watched the world trickle past. Then, after locking *Rosie*, he set off for New Scotland Yard and his own personal fiefdom, the Black Museum.

The Yard has two separate Black Museums. One is a training college for new recruits to the Force. Inside this

Black Museum is a selection of original hangman's nooses and the Death Masks of some of London's worst deviants. There are knives and shotguns, all behind glass of course, and pictures of criminals that terrorised the city. On the 7th floor of the New Scotland Yard building is another Black Museum. It accepts no visitors and offers no tours. In this place are the damned souls and the demon spirits of killers, poisoners, rapists, murderers, and the foulest of the foul. They are all locked up inside their own personal purgatories, and Judas Iscariot is their warder and occasional tormentor.

The journey to the Yard was uneventful. Judas kept looking over his shoulder though because he had the feeling that he was being followed, but that proved to be a mild paranoia. He entered the lift on the ground floor and, as usual, it had vacated before he pushed the button for the 7th floor. The rank and file, although brave and wonderful people who thought nothing of running into danger to protect the innocent, drew the line at sharing the lift with the strange DCI from the Black Museum.

Judas alighted from the lift, wandered down the corridor to his office, unlocked the door and stepped inside. Fortunately, there were no angels sitting on the window ledge waiting for him or ghosts floating around and interfering with his filing, so Judas decided to make himself a cup of coffee. To his horror, he found he had used the last of his special supply. He was a coffee snob and always got his beans from an odd little man in town who had a direct link to a grower in the Levant, which was the only place that Judas believed produced decent coffee beans. So, Judas had to make do with instant coffee granules. A poor start to any day in his book.

He took his mug of steaming brown flavoured water and one of the orange Hob Nob biscuits he had liberated from his friend and colleague Bloody Nora's secret stash, and sat down and went through his mail. After that, he checked on the Black Museum. The artefacts and the exhibits were all calm and minding their own business. Millie the Manticore and her ghostly friend Emily, who were Judas's assistants and also fledgling detectives, were absent. Hopefully, they were staying out of trouble and keeping an eye on things in the Time Fields, so Judas returned to his office and started to think about last night's impromptu attack by busker Bosk.

There was something clearly amiss here. Something that he wasn't seeing. In his experience, there was always a rhythm to most cases. Everything was slow and pedestrian at the beginning, and then things accelerated and if you weren't in charge of the wheel or the brakes, accidents happened, and lives were lost. So, Judas went back over the sequence of events. The first thing to consider was Cat Tabby. That little mischief-maker had come to him voluntarily and told him all about this unusual waif that he'd discovered wandering the mean streets of London. The boy had been in contact with something from the realms of the Fae. Cat Tabby had suggested that it might be something like a Siren.

Cat Tabby had never volunteered anything in his whole, long and colourful life. He had also made sure to mention a reward. Of course he had. Judas was beginning to wonder if the slinky feline had more than one paw in the litter tray, as it were. Then there was the Siren. The beast had already attacked two young men in central London. Killing and eating one, seriously injuring the other. The Chief Super of the Met would be on his case about that soon enough.

So, on reflection, Judas had a Missing Person, or rather a

lost boy who had been touched by magic, a ravenous and dangerous Siren, a Woodland Sprite called Bosk, and the annoying but ever-present Cat Tabby, all involved in what appeared to be the same affair. Or were they?

Judas sat down behind his desk and reached into his pocket for his silver coin. The ancient Roman sliver of silver, one of thirty for services rendered long ago, was now reduced to nothing more than a metal wafer so thin that it was almost transparent, and the details, once so clear – the Aquiline nose and the laurels – were now but scratchy lines on the surface. He sat back in his creaky familiar chair and started to rub his thumb around the edge of the coin in slow, regular clockwise movements until his breathing slowed, his eyelids dropped, and he fell back into the past and his memories.

When Judas awoke, the hour hand on the clock on the wall had sprinted past the number 12. He sat up and pocketed the coin. He felt refreshed, and his mind was clearer than it had been. Judas needed to concentrate on the boy. So, he went through the Missing Persons reports. There had been a shocking rise in the number of young people going missing in the last year alone. Judas looked at their faces as their files appeared on his screen, and he felt sorry for them. Truly sorry.

After an hour of searching, he had a shortlist. It was depressingly long for a shortlist, but it was a start. He continued to refine and reduce the list until he had a handful of young men that he thought were viable options. He was about to send the list down to the front desk where it would be divided among the constables on the beat who would be his eyes and ears on the street, when he noticed that there had been a request from Interpol for information regarding the disappearance of the son of the British

Ambassador in Oslo. Judas clicked on the file and the image of a young man called Sid appeared. He was the right age... and the last sighting of him had been in a forest just outside Oslo at the ceremony of the cutting down of the Norwegian Christmas tree prior to its transportation to Trafalgar Square.

22

ESCAPE

Bosk was feeling edgy and uncomfortable as he approached Trafalgar Square. He had arranged to meet with the talking cat there to see if it had found the boy yet. The cat was nowhere to be seen, so Bosk approached the tree and waited for it to appear. He thought about taking out his fiddle and playing some music to cheer himself up, but he was not in the mood. Something didn't feel right, and he couldn't put his finger on it.

Heldra was in her tree. She had sensed the Woodland Sprite and saw Bosk coming towards her, but just as he reached her tree, he moved off to one side and sat down on an empty bench. He looked thoughtful.

"Why is he just sitting there and waiting? He could just use that infernal fiddle to put everyone to sleep, and then he could try to catch and kill me," she hissed.

Bosk caught Heldra's scent then. It was the same musky and pungent mix of flesh and blood that he had first smelt in the forest on the island of Hisoy all those years ago, and he knew she was near. His head came up and he scanned the crowd, but he had a feeling that she was looking right at him at that very moment. The only place that she would feel comfortable hiding was in the tree.

Heldra saw Bosk's head lift, and then the interfering little monster turned around and looked directly at the branches she was hiding in. Heldra hissed again and made a break for it.

Bosk saw Heldra leap from the tree. She had obviously been using her time well as she rested up. The Siren had taken stock of her surroundings and had planned her escape route. She landed, took two steps and then jumped onto the roof of one of the pop-up bars. From there, she leaped onto the empty plinth and then, with one colossal bound, she jumped onto the roof of the National Portrait Gallery and disappeared from view.

Heldra scrambled onto the roof of the vast building with the flags outside it. There, she hid behind a grey box with a doorway set on one side and waited for Bosk to come for her.

23

A BOY, A CAT AND A REWARD

Sid had wasted no time in getting from Shooter's Hill to Trafalgar Square. A flatbed lorry carrying hundreds of metal poles, stacks of scaffolding boards and two lads from the Isle of Sheppey had stopped at a set of lights and offered Sid a lift. The snow had really started coming down, and they had wanted to do someone a good turn. Fortunately for him, that someone was Sid. They dropped him off just outside Tottenham Court Road tube station and gave him the directions to get to the square. Sid tried to pay the lads for their kindness with his expensive snowboarding jacket, but they refused him.

Cat Tabby was padding through the snow. He liked this time of year – the sounds, the sights, the smells of roasted chestnuts – and the increased gullibility of the general public because it was Christmas time and the season of goodwill to all men.

'Humbug!' thought Cat Tabby.

He was on his way down to Trafalgar Square from Leicester Square, weaving through the tourist-free streets and roads, humming to himself and thinking about the size of the fee he would charge for his services. Of course it should be big! Why not? After all, he was saving a young man from spending the festive season on the cold and dangerous streets of London. But then a thought crept into Cat Tabby's large and devious mind, and it warmed him from claw to swishing tail. He was going to get a payment from this Woodland Sprite Bosk to locate the boy for him. One payment. Why didn't he give DCI Judas Iscariot the same information and get paid twice? Bosk would not have been able to get rid of Judas, after all.

Sid walked to the bottom of Charing Cross Road, crossing over and into Trafalgar Square when he reached the church of St-Martin-in-the-Fields. As he walked, he kept seeing the faces of the same few people he had seen in the strange campervan in the woods. Cat Tabby saw Sid at precisely the same time that he saw DCI Judas Iscariot appear outside the Waterstones bookstore at the top of Northumberland Avenue and nearly leaped into the air. He had a quick decision to make. He was banking on keeping the boy quiet in Oxleas Woodlands for at least another day, but here he was! Cat Tabby needed to act fast.

"Inspector! Inspector!" shouted Cat Tabby.

Judas saw Cat Tabby and walked towards him.

"Funny seeing you here," said Judas.

"Funny wasn't the word I'd use, Inspector. Fortunate is the word I would use. I have located the boy and I am ready to collect the reward you mentioned," said Cat Tabby.

"We discussed a reward, Cat Tabby, I don't remember settling on a figure though," said Judas.

Cat Tabby was acting strangely. Judas could see that he was trying to guide him away from the Christmas Tree for some reason.

"Are you okay?" Judas asked.

"Perfectly well, Inspector. Why don't you catch your breath here, and I shall fetch the lad," said Cat Tabby.

Judas looked up and scanned the crowd. A boy wearing a fancy snowboarding jacket was heading towards the tree and he looked familiar. Cat Tabby had also seen him.

"Why! What a stroke of luck! I was due to meet him later, but there he is! Just over there, Inspector," said Cat Tabby.

"What an incredible stroke of luck," said Judas.

Cat Tabby sprinted away towards the boy.

"Hello again, you look well rested," said Cat Tabby.

Sid looked down at the cat.

"You locked me in!" he said.

"Put you somewhere safe, you mean," said Cat Tabby.

"It didn't feel that way," said Sid.

Judas approached them, took out his Warrant Card and showed it to Sid.

"Hello, Sid. My name is Detective Chief Inspector Judas Iscariot of Scotland Yard," said Judas.

Sid looked at the card and then into Judas's face, as the first tear rolled down his cheek. But there was no time for further introductions or explanations because that's when the screaming started.

24

FANGS AND A FIDDLE

Bosk was panting heavily. He had a long bloody gash running down his side, and part of the little finger on his right hand was missing. Heldra was lying motionless on the far side of the roof. A pool of blood was growing around her head like some dark halo. They had fought each other across the roof and back, and at one point Bosk thought he was finished. The Siren was immensely strong and ferocious, but she was not used to being attacked by music. The first tune he had played had knocked all the wind from her and sent her reeling, but she had regained her feet before he had a chance to play the next and caught him with a raking slash of her talons.

But Bosk was the more powerful spirit, and he had collected many songs and melodies that could either protect or harm, and it was only a matter of time before he brought Heldra down. He was just about to hum a healing tune when the man in the smart blue suit appeared.

Judas heard the screams and saw the people pointing to the top of the National Portrait Gallery. He also saw the Siren in her true form, fox tail and all, clamber up the wall and disappear onto the roof. Seconds later, he saw Bosk running after her.

"You two! Stay right here. Do not move, especially not you," shouted Judas.

Cat Tabby looked hurt, and Sid just looked bewildered. Judas ran to the entrance to the gallery and disappeared inside. When he got to the top of the main stairwell, he barged through the fire door at the top of a short flight of steps and onto the roof. The first thing he saw was the Siren. She was badly hurt and lying in a puddle of what appeared to be her own blood. Bosk was standing on the other side of the roof, and he looked as though he were about to fall to his knees and pass out.

"Stop! Right now! Put your fiddle down on the ground and make it slow!" shouted Judas.

Bosk saw only the man that the cat had called a murderer and acted instinctively to defend himself. He lifted his fiddle and placed it under his chin. Judas quickly reached for his secret weapons and placed them in his ears. Judas was not much of a music lover but he did have a Spotify account. After being caught by surprise once by the pesky Woodland Sprite, Judas had taken steps to make sure that he was not caught out again. He turned up the volume on his phone and ran towards Bosk. The look on the Woodland Sprite's face was one of confusion when Judas reached him. He'd been playing a crushing melody that should have brought the man to his knees, but he was unaffected and still coming. Judas reached Bosk and then casually punched him so hard in the face that Bosk's feet left the ground for a second. When the sprite hit the ground, he was out for the count.

25

A PRESENT AT CHRISTMAS

Sid was sitting on a large brown leather sofa at the back of an office in New Scotland Yard with a cup of excellent coffee in hand. Judas had already made the calls to Interpol and the British Ambassador's Residence in Oslo. The first call was perfunctory and short. The second call was longer and more emotional. Sid had regained some of his memory, although not much. When Judas had shown him his own picture, courtesy of the Interpol files, he had wept because he finally remembered his name. Judas then showed him the images of his mother and father from the UK Government website. It was going to take Sid a long time to fully remember what had happened to him over the past few weeks. In a way, Judas hoped he wouldn't remember the bits with Sirens, talking cats, and Tardis-like VW Campervans in the middle of the woods. But that was not something he could control.

Two hours later, a member of the Government Liaison Staff arrived to collect the boy. Judas took Sid downstairs to the foyer, signed the paperwork, and saw Sid on his way. The lad looked exhausted, and Judas expected him to sleep on the plane home. When he returned to the 7th floor, Judas was not surprised to find Cat Tabby sitting on the window ledge again.

"Evening, Inspector. I presume the Land Rover Discovery with the blacked-out windows that arrived just five minutes ago was for that poor little lad," said Cat Tabby.

Judas just looked at him. It was as if butter wouldn't melt in that cat's mouth. He was so brazen and unashamed that Judas had to laugh.

"*That poor little lad*? Absolutely outrageous, even for you," said Judas.

Cat Tabby raised a paw and placed it over his heart.

"Inspector! How could you? I found that boy, lost and alone and then took him in and kept him safe, just like you wanted me to. I even brought him to you directly," said Cat Tabby.

Judas had to marvel at the performance.

"I believe you. Millions wouldn't. Anyway, if you came to see your dear friend off, you've just missed him," said Judas.

"Oh, what a shame. I'll write to him. Keep in touch. Pen-pals, that's what we'll become," said Cat Tabby.

"I'm very happy for you both. Now, if there isn't anything else? I'd like to get on, I have some Christmas shopping to do," said Judas.

Cat Tabby hopped from the ledge and sidled up to Judas.

"Well, there was one last thing I had hoped to finalise with you. The reward? When can I expect it?" said Cat Tabby.

Judas looked down into the little con-cat's face.

"If I thought that I could get you off my back, I would just open that window and toss you out, but you did come and tell me about the lad. That's something, I suppose.

Leave it with me. I will make another call to Oslo and see what's what," said Judas.

"That's very magnanimous of you, Inspector. I shall return. Oh, and by the way, Happy Christmas, Inspector. I imagine that this is a very lonely time for you, all things considered," said Cat Tabby.

"I'm going to go and make myself a coffee, so don't be here when I get back," said Judas.

"Ho! Ho! Ho!" cried Cat Tabby before jumping back up onto the window ledge and disappearing.

Judas did not go to the galley kitchen at all. Instead, he went into the Black Museum. He had asked Millie the Manticore to keep an eye on the Siren, and if the beast woke up and wanted to cause any trouble, Millie would gently remind her to behave sensibly. But as soon as he entered the Key Room, he knew that the Siren had died. Millie had done her best, but the Siren had taken a real beating from Bosk and lost far too much blood on the roof of the National Portrait Gallery.

Bosk had regained consciousness an hour after Judas had brought him to the Black Museum. He was groggy and in pain from the wound that Heldra had given him, but the Woodland Sprite saw someone had dressed his wound. He realised he was not in any immediate danger and agreed to cooperate with Judas, especially after he was informed that his fiddle and bow had been confiscated.

Bosk told Judas his story, and Judas filled in the gaps with what he had heard from Cat Tabby. As far as Judas was concerned Bosk had tried to do a good thing, and Judas told him he was free to leave whenever he felt able. Millie volunteered to remove the Siren's dead body for him. Judas agreed, but shortly after giving her permission, it occurred to him that Millie had no intention of handing the body of the beast over to Bloody Nora at all. Millie was always hungry, after all.

Later that night, after Judas had written his report for the Chief Super and returned Bosk's fiddle to him, he realised it was Christmas Eve.

Judas thanked Emily and Millie, said goodbye to Bosk and took the lift down to the ground floor. There were balloons and bunting everywhere. One constable had dressed up as Santa Claus, carols and festive tunes were playing over the PA system, and the tree in the corner was still standing, at least for now. Judas left the station and walked down to the Embankment. The fallen snow was still white and compact instead of grey and slushy, and London looked stunning. He took a cab back to Little Venice and *Rosie,* and was surprised to find that someone, or something, had left two Christmas presents for him. One was a hamper from Fortnum & Mason. The other was a new generator with a red bow on top.

26

OSLO

Sid woke up in a bed that he knew was his. It felt right, and when he rolled over onto his side, there was already a dip that fitted his shoulder perfectly. He looked at the clock on the bedside table and saw that it was already 10.30am, so he hopped out of bed, showered, and dressed. When he got downstairs, he found the man and the woman who had greeted him the night before waiting for him. They had been told that Sid had lost his memory but that it would return in time, so they were gentle and patient with him, and he, in turn, was careful not to upset them.

The family sat down to breakfast, and then Sid's parents gave him their gifts. Sid's mother had never given up hope of having him home for Christmas and had bought him presents as usual. In her mind, not buying them would have been tantamount to giving up on him. They ate a fantastic Christmas Day dinner and watched a lot of old movies in front of the fire. Sid's parents fell asleep during *Die Hard*, but he felt he had slept far too much already so he put a blanket over them both and went to make himself a sandwich. When he entered the kitchen, someone was waiting for him.

"Hello, Sid," said Cat Tabby.

END

ABOUT THE AUTHOR

Martin studied Art at the Central Saint Martin's School of Art in Covent Garden. He later ventured into the world of advertising, serving as a copywriter and creative director at some of London's most renowned agencies. He has lived and worked in Amsterdam and Barcelona.

He has driven a speedboat on the Costa Del Crime, peeled onions for pasties in Devon, erected scaffolding all over London, and now writes full-time.

He lives in Kent with his wife, two children, and their English Bulldog, Boba, named after the deadliest bounty hunter from a galaxy far, far away.

 facebook.com/martdavey
 instagram.com/martdaveyauthor

ALSO BY MARTIN DAVEY

Judas the Hero

The Children of the Lightning

Oliver Twisted

The Blind Beak of Bow Street

The Curious Case of Cat Tabby

The Death of the Black Museum

The Murder of the Mudlarks

An Ink So Dark

A Burning in the Heavens

The Lords of Under

The Coming of the Darkest Raven

A Quiet Sphere of Chaos

AFTERWORD

If you've enjoyed this book, please do consider leaving a review of it on the Amazon website. Even a few positive words can make a massive difference to independent authors like me, so I'd be delighted and grateful if you'd show your appreciation.

Many thanks, Martin

Printed in Great Britain
by Amazon